CREATIVE WOMAN MYSTERIES®

Deadly
Garland

Elizabeth Blair

Annie's®

AnniesFiction.com

Library of Congress-in-Publication Data
Deadly Garland / Elizabeth Blair
p. cm.
I. Title
2013918634

CreativeWomanMysteries.com
800-282-6643
Creative Woman Mysteries®
Series Editors: Ken and Janice Tate

10 11 12 13 14 | Printed in China | 9 8 7 6 5 4 3 2

— 1 —

Shannon McClain slit open the cardboard box with a utility knife, an excited smile on her face. "Wait until you see the Christmas stocking kits I found, Essie. Our customers are going to love them."

Store manager Essie Engleman joined her at the counter of the Paisley Craft Market & Artist Lofts, eager to view the new merchandise. All around them, the shop gave evidence of the season: a display of gorgeous handmade ornaments, green garland and tiny lights outlining the windows, and a floor strewn with the boxes of Christmas craft projects Essie was putting away on racks and shelves. Orchestral Christmas carols played softly in the background.

Shannon pulled out several of the felt stocking appliqué kits featuring snowmen and spread them out on the counter. "Aren't they cute?"

Essie studied one with two snowmen on skates. "They sure are. I can think of several people who are going to snap them right up."

"Let me check this order, and then I'll help you put away everything. We open in fifteen minutes."

Essie gave a rueful shrug. "Yeah. I'd better get some of this stuff off the floor before customers trip over it." She went back to the nearest pile and began to slide cellophane bags containing Christmas beads onto hooks. "These beads are giving me ideas for projects," she said. Essie made bead jewelry in addition to being a wonderful chalk artist. As part of her salary, she received free use of an artist loft upstairs. Shannon rented the others to various crafters.

Shannon found the inventory statement from the vendor tucked inside the box and confirmed the goods received against it. Hearing an odd noise from the street, she cocked her head. *What was that?* She turned down the sound system and listened. *There it is again.*

"Help! Somebody help me!"

"Do you hear that, Essie?" Shannon asked, running to the front door and peering out. "Someone is calling for help." She didn't see anything, so she unlocked the door and stepped out into the cool, foggy morning. Essie was right behind her.

This time of day, before most of the stores on Apple Grove's Main Street opened, there were very few cars or pedestrians around. Just up the street was a van parked beside a pickup truck, and Shannon heard the cries once again from that direction.

She bolted up the sidewalk toward the voice. Once past the truck, she saw the victim. A heavyset, middle-aged man with a cast on his right leg lay sprawled on the pavement beside the van. The open side door and the wheelchair just beyond his reach told the story. He must have tried to get into his chair and had fallen.

"Don't just gawk at me, girl. Help me up!" he snapped at Shannon. From under beetled brows, he shot her a ferocious glare. But the twist of his mouth, almost hidden by a heavy beard, revealed he was in pain.

A wave of compassion flooding her, she hurried toward him. "Of course. That's why we're here."

Essie moved the wheelchair into place as Shannon positioned herself behind the man. Shannon pulled up from under his left arm while Essie lifted from the right; together, with the man using his good leg, they were able to propel him up and into his chair.

"That's better," he said with a relieved sigh. "Thanks. Sorry I was so short with you."

"Do we need to call a doctor?" Essie asked, patting his shoulder.

"No. I'm fine."

"Are you here by yourself?" Shannon asked, wondering what to do next.

"Of course not," he said. "He was supposed to take five minutes, but he's as slow as molasses in January. And it's only December."

Shannon exchanged a glance with Essie. Who was he talking about? Before she could probe further, quick footsteps tapped along the sidewalk. A good-looking young man appeared around the front of the pickup, stopping dead when he caught sight of the trio. "Dick! What happened? I told you to wait for me." His blue eyes were somber with concern. Like Dick, he was dressed in a tan canvas work jacket, matching pants, knit wool cap, and rubber-soled boots.

"I fell down while trying to get in this darn-fool chair. It got away from me. These kind ladies helped me out."

"I'm Shannon McClain," she said, holding her hand out to Dick and the younger man. "I own the Paisley Craft Market. And this is Essie Engleman, my manager."

"Pleased to meet you both," the young man said, a broad grin breaking out across his handsome, square-jawed face.

"I'm Gary Booker, and this old man is my boss, Dick Olson of Olson's Tree Farm." His hand lingered in Essie's, Shannon noticed. "We were just on our way to see you. Dick's wife placed a yarn order, and we're here to pick it up."

"Let's go in then," Shannon said. "Coffee is on me."

Shannon settled Dick and Gary in the attached coffee shop, Espresso Yourself, and while Essie put together their drink requests, Shannon located Marge Olson's yarn order. She'd chosen a gorgeous, heathery blue-green lace yarn. Shorn from baby alpaca, the ultrafine fiber was soft and fluffy, perfect for cloud-like shawls or scarves. Lace knitting was an intricate and painstaking process, and Shannon admired anyone attempting it.

The front doorbell jingled and Carrie Weston, one of the shop's employees, came in. "Good morning, Shannon," she said, taking off her hat and shaking the moisture from the fog out of her dark hair. "Did you hear? We might get snow."

Essie's laugh rang out in the coffee shop.

"What's going on?" Carrie asked.

"Oh, we had a little excitement today," Shannon replied. "Dick Olson fell trying to get into his wheelchair and Essie and I helped him up. He and Gary Booker are having coffee while I put together—"

"Gary's here?" Carrie's eyes widened. Without stopping to take off her coat, she scurried into the coffee shop. Curious, Shannon followed, the bagged yarn order in her hand.

Essie was behind the counter and Gary was leaning against it while Dick sat in his chair nearby. "Hi, Carrie," Essie said, beaming. "Do you know Dick Olson and Gary Booker?"

"Yes, I do." Carrie walked over to Gary and put her hand on his arm. "Hi. So nice of you to come see me at work."

"Uh ... yeah. We had to pick up yarn for Marge, and I hoped I'd see you." Now he turned the full wattage of his grin on her. They put their heads together, whispering.

Her face falling, Essie turned away and began to tidy up the prep area. "Want a coffee, Shannon?" she asked. All traces of laughter were gone from her voice.

"No, thanks. I'm fine right now." Shannon crossed the room and handed Dick the bag. "Here's Marge's yarn. She already paid, so you're all set." She pulled up a chair and sat beside him. "Is your leg feeling all right?"

He grunted. "It's OK. My foolishness didn't hurt it any, thank goodness."

"What happened, if I may ask?"

"Had an ATV accident out at the farm. Good thing Gary was around. Slid into a ditch, fell off, and lay there for quite a while." Words trailing off, he stared into space.

Shannon watched him with concern, hoping he didn't have a concussion.

Gary looked around. "Guess it's time we get going, old man. Got a lot of trees that need cutting." He winked at Shannon, running long fingers through his thick blond hair before tugging the knit cap back on. "Our big season kicks off this weekend."

The man was attractive, she had to admit. "Oh, really?"

"Yes, ma'am. We do Christmas trees. The best in the state. Come see us, and I'll give you a discount." He gave Carrie a friendly one-armed hug and said, "See you later, babe."

Essie rolled her eyes.

Gary nodded at Essie and Shannon. "Nice to meet you both. Thanks again for your help. And the coffee."

"I thank you," Dick said, "and the wife thanks you." He shook the bag of yarn for emphasis, then tucked it securely beside his good leg before wheeling toward the front door. As he moved forward, Gary followed, making sure he didn't bump anything and then hustling forward to open the door.

Once the door slammed behind them, Essie turned to Carrie. "We've got tons of merchandise to get on the shelves, so let's get going." She ducked around the counter and stalked back into the main shop.

"OK then." Carrie replied with an eye roll of her own, throwing off her coat as she followed Essie.

Shannon sighed. At times like this, even doing paperwork was appealing. She escaped to the office to work on the bank deposit.

A little later, she looked up to see Essie in the doorway. "Everything all right out there?"

Nodding, Essie came into the office and collapsed into a chair. "We've got all the new stock put away, and now we're rearranging some of the old stuff."

"And?" Shannon raised one brow.

Essie smiled. "Oh, the Gary thing? Carrie told me she's been dating him for a while. And he's a huge flirt. So we're good." She shuddered. "I don't want a guy like that anyway. How can you trust him?"

You can't.

Shannon zipped the bank bag. "I'm going to the bank now to beat the lunch rush. When I come back, you two can take turns going out for lunch. I brought some of Deborah's leftover seafood chowder to heat up." Deborah Waters had been cook and confidant for Shannon's grandmother, Victoria Paisley. When Shannon inherited the craft market and the Paisley mansion, Deborah had stayed on.

"Yum," Essie said, getting up. "It's a perfect day for chowder."

Outside, the fog had lifted but the sky was still overcast. Maybe it *would* snow—a rare but not unheard-of event in the Pacific Northwest. Shannon sauntered along the sidewalk, enjoying the sharp, cold air. Up ahead, two men from the town crew were attaching a giant snowflake to a lamppost. The lamps on the other side of the street were already adorned with snowflakes, stars, and angels, and Shannon could picture how at night the gas lamps would glow in the center of the lit decorations. Oversize candy canes trimmed the edges of the green, and in the center, an enormous fir tree awaited the tree-lighting ceremony. Most of the shopkeepers along Main Street had filled their flower boxes with evergreens, berries, and seasonal ornaments; many had outlined the windows and doors and cornices of their brick and clapboard buildings with strings of lights. One leafless tree was even hung with jumbo globes, a delightful touch.

Picturesque Apple Grove, Oregon, was just as popular in the winter as summer, with visitors enjoying shopping and themed events. For Shannon, this year was shaping up to be a memorable one. The twins, Alec and Lara, would be home; her mother, Beth, was back in her life; and Michael ... well, it would be wonderful to share the Christmas holidays with him. In addition, the market was doing really well, especially since she had opened the coffee shop. Her steps quickened. She had to take care of the banking and get back.

In this season, even the bank's dull tan decor looked festive. Someone with a lavish hand had adorned the counters and desks with red-and-gold garlands, bows, and balls. A huge wreath hung on the glass wall of bank manager Bill Buchanan's office, almost blocking the view of Bill meeting with two men inside.

Shannon studied the wreath as she waited in line to make the deposit. *I should add wreath-making supplies to the inventory. Maybe offer a class.* After finishing her transaction at the teller window, she took a seat near Bill's office to wait for him. From there she could see past the wreath into the office, and she recognized the men. Dick Olson and Gary Booker. As she watched, Bill handed Gary several small white cards. Shannon had signed identical ones when she opened her bank accounts. After Gary signed each card, he handed it to Dick, who also signed. Feeling like a snoop, she glanced away. It was none of her business if Dick Olson was giving Gary access to his money. After all, she trusted Essie with cashing out the registers.

Then she thought of Morgan Lombardi, the craft store manager who had been in place when she arrived in Apple Grove. The clues had been subtle, but Shannon remembered sensing that Morgan wasn't trustworthy. Gary somehow aroused the same feelings. Although on the surface he was solicitous, calling Dick "the old man" had seemed disrespectful. Despite his generally gruff nature, Dick seemed too feeble to challenge Gary.

The door to Bill's office opened, and he ushered out his customers. "Thanks again, gentlemen. And let me know if you need anything else." His gaze fell on Shannon. "Here to see me?"

"Yes, I am, if you have time." Gary and Dick nodded to Shannon as they exited Bill's office.

"Just give me a minute," Bill said. "I've got a call on hold."

Shannon watched Gary and Dick make their way across the lobby, Dick grumbling about their remaining errands. To her discomfort, she witnessed Gary roll his eyes and throw his hands up in mock exasperation behind Dick's back. One of the pretty tellers giggled.

Shannon shook her head, wondering briefly how Gary managed to have so many people eating out of his hand. Then she returned to contemplating her plans for the holidays while she waited for Bill.

2

The rest of the day was busy with people looking for Christmas crafts, and seven o'clock found Shannon tired but exhilarated as she made coffee and tea for the Purls of Hope knitting group meeting. If this pace kept up, she would need to order more inventory. She hoped the suppliers would still have some available.

The store bell jingled and Joyce Buchanan, Bill's wife and the owner of Pink Sprinkles Bakery, entered. "It's getting cold out there," she said with a shiver, placing a big pink bakery box with black polka dots on the stone counter.

"What did you bring us?" Shannon asked, opening the box. Inside, two dozen powdered-sugar balls sat nestled in bakery paper.

Joyce unwound the fuchsia scarf covering her platinum-blond bob before answering. In her mid-forties, Joyce always wore bright pink; tonight the scarf matched her lipstick and the cozy cashmere turtleneck she had paired with black wool pants. "Chocolate wedding-cake cookies. I want the Purls to test them for my Twelve Days of Christmas Cookies event." She took off her coat and tucked the scarf into a sleeve.

"I'll test any cookies anytime," Shannon said with a laugh. She pulled out a stack of small plates and set them beside the box.

Melanie and Betty were next to arrive, each carrying a

lush red poinsettia. "We come bearing gifts!" Melanie sang out. "We just got a shipment in."

"Thank you so much," Shannon said. "Let's put one on the front counter and one in here." Both pots held a florist's card advertising The Flower Pot, where Melanie worked. Apple Grove's downtown businesses often promoted one another.

"Wow. Those are beautiful," Joyce said. "Can you get them in pink?"

"Sure can," Melanie said, taking off her coat and putting it on the back of her chair. "We also have white and burgundy available."

"I'd like some for the inn," Betty commented, returning from the main shop, where she had placed the plant. Betty and her husband ran The Apple Grove Inn. "What are we making tonight?" The Purls of Hope knitted garments, blankets, and accessories for charity.

Shannon set a large basket of brightly colored yarns on a table. "I told Pastor Boyer we'd make pompom hats and mittens for the Angel Tree. They'll go to needy children." Pastor Rodney Boyer was the minister at the First Methodist Church, which Shannon and the others attended.

"That sounds fun," Joyce said. "Quick too. I should be able to make several sets." They gathered around the basket, selecting yarn, needles, and a copy of the pattern Shannon had printed.

"Are we late?" Kate Ellis, the youngest member of the group and owner of Ultimutt Grooming, a dog-grooming shop, came into the room. "I hope you don't mind." Kate swung her long dark ponytail as she nodded toward her companion. "I brought Hillary Jenkins with me. I thought she might like to meet some people."

As Kate stepped farther into the coffee shop, Shannon saw her companion. Hillary was short with curly blond hair that hung in her eyes and glasses that slid down her nose. She wore baggy clothes in dull colors that gave an impression of depression and gloom. Giving a little wave in response to Kate's introduction, she shuffled forward as though uncertain of her welcome.

Another of Kate's strays. Kate had a soft spot for even the most unattractive and difficult dogs, and that seemed to extend to humans as well. Quickly clamping down on the thought as uncharitable, Shannon smiled in greeting. "Please do come in. Have a seat."

"Glad to meet you, Hillary," Joyce said warmly. "Are you new to town?"

Kate answered for her. "Yes. She's temping at the shop since I've been so busy lately." She settled Hillary in a chair, placing the girl's army-surplus backpack beside her. "Want coffee?"

Hillary nodded. "Thanks for including me even though I can't knit," she said in a low voice.

"That's not a problem," Betty said, bringing the yarn basket over. "We'll teach you."

Everyone settled into the soft leather chairs with their projects, cups of coffee or tea, and plates of cookies close at hand. Kate showed Hillary how to cast on, and she laboriously began to knit her first stitches, frowning in concentration.

"The town is really looking festive," Shannon commented. "Apple Grove really celebrates Christmas in a big way."

"We sure do," Betty said. "We get a lot of tourists this

time of year, believe it or not. I'm all booked up for Christmas week already."

"Next week is the tree-lighting ceremony," Melanie put
in. "The official kickoff of the season. All the stores are decorating and rolling out their special promotions."

"Speaking of which," Joyce said, "how do you like
the cookies?"

They all murmured their appreciation. Betty mentioned
that the chocolate was a surprise since most wedding-cake
cookies were nut-flavored.

"I still need to get Christmas trees," Shannon said. "I
want one for here as well as at home."

"Olson's Tree Farm is the place to go," Joyce said. "They're
just outside town and they have the best trees. Marge Olson
was a good friend of your grandmother's, by the way." She
sighed and shook her head. "The Olsons have had more than
their share of problems, but Marge is a real trouper."

"What a coincidence!" Shannon exclaimed. "I met her
husband, Dick, today. He and his employee, Gary Booker,
came into the shop for a yarn order."

"Spit!" Hillary's voice was the loudest she'd used yet. As
they all looked at her, she added sheepishly, "Sorry. I just
messed up."

"Oh, we all do that once in a while," Betty reassured her.

Kate helped Hillary pick up the dropped stitch while
Shannon related how Dick had fallen. "Do you know Gary?"
she asked the group, hoping to hear something positive to
outweigh her negative impression. If he was trouble, she
was concerned for Carrie, who seemed quite attached already. Not that it was really her business.

They all shook their heads. "He must be new," Betty said.

"Well, he's a handsome one," Shannon said. "I have to give him that. He got my girls all aflutter with his flirting."

"Oh, introduce me!" Kate said. "I could stand to meet someone handsome. It's been too long since I've been on a date."

The others hooted at Kate's frankness.

"Nice is better than handsome," Betty remarked. "Handsome is as handsome does."

"That's right," Hillary said. "Take it from me." Her grim tone fell like a stone plopping into a pond, quieting the group for a moment.

What's her story? Shannon studied Hillary, hunched over her knitting in a protective posture, her clumsy fingers fumbling with the needles.

Then Joyce rallied. "Sometimes we're lucky and get both. I did and so did you, Betty. And Michael is definitely good-looking, isn't he, Shannon?"

Shannon blushed, thinking of the dark-haired, blue-eyed security consultant who had gradually made his way into her heart. "Och, away with you!" She changed the subject. "I've been thinking about offering wreath-making classes. I saw a fantastic one at the bank today on Bill's office window that inspired me. What do you all think?"

"I usually buy a wreath for the front door of the inn," Betty said, "but it would be fun to make my own. Count me in."

"I can bring pinecones and holly berries and seedpods from the shop for decorations," Melanie said. "And floral wire."

"Wonderful. We already have ribbon for bows here," Shannon went on. "And I can get frames from my supplier. Maybe the Olsons sell evergreen boughs as well as trees."

"They do," Joyce put in.

"Perfect," Shannon said. "Now I just need an instructor. Do any of you know how to make wreaths?"

"I do," Hillary said. "I ... um ... used to work with plants at a nursery. We did wreaths and dried-flower arrangements all the time."

Shannon looked at her in surprise, having assumed the girl had no craft interests.

"Hillary's got a good eye," Kate said, a note of pride in her voice. "Look at her backpack."

Obediently they all studied the olive-green pack, which indeed held dozens of bright and colorful patches and pins arranged in an eye-catching pattern. Shannon saw emblems in simple geometric shapes as well as some depicting various indoor and outdoor activities. "Those remind me of the Girl Guides in Scotland," she said. "I used to be a member. We worked to get badges and pins."

"That's right," Hillary said. "They're vintage Girl Scout badges. I collect them."

It was quickly arranged that Hillary would teach wreath making later in the week. Shannon made plans to go out to the farm the next morning with Betty and Kate to buy trees and order cut boughs. Soon after, the meeting broke up, and Shannon shooed everyone out, claiming that cleaning up would help her unwind after a busy day.

She washed the cups and saucers, put the rest of the cookies in the pastry case, and bagged up the garbage. Making a circuit of the room, she arranged the tables and chairs back in their usual positions. Hillary had left her knitting on her chair, and Shannon picked up the little piece, consisting of three rows of twisted, knotted yarn. *I'm sure she's more adept at handling evergreen boughs,* Shannon thought with a smile as she put the knitting behind the counter.

Outside, the air was indeed much colder than it had been earlier in the day, as Joyce had said. Carrying the bag of garbage, she picked her way carefully across the drive toward the dumpster. The back-door light illuminated only a small radius, and once outside its glow, the area was pitch black. She really should remember to bring a flashlight out here.

Halfway to the dumpster, she heard a strange noise and paused. *What was that?* There it was again. Something rustled in the pile of cardboard boxes next to the dumpster.

3

Shannon's pulse quickened. Was someone lying in wait to attack her? Nonsense. It was too cold for muggers to lurk and well past the time she usually brought garbage out. *Too many mysteries and close calls in the past couple of years*, she thought. The rustling came again, and she called out, "Who's there?" If they didn't answer, she decided, she'd take the garbage back inside and dispose of it in the morning.

She was just about ready to do that when she spotted eyes glowing green among the boxes. Relief swept through her. It was only an animal, and by the size, she guessed it was a dog.

That suspicion was confirmed by the tapping of toenails on the pavement as the creature moved toward her. When he drew closer, the dim light revealed the thick, golden fur of a retriever mix.

"What are you doing out here?" she asked as the dog sniffed and pawed at the garbage bag. "Don't you have a home?" She continued to the dumpster and threw the bag in. The dog followed, sniffing the ground for any dropped morsels.

As she opened the back door, the dog still at her heels, he sat down and whined, big brown eyes pleading. "All right. I'll give you some water and something to eat. But it won't be dog food," she warned. A few minutes later, after locking up the store, she carried out a bowl of water and a couple of bran muffins. "At least they're healthy," she said, patting his fuzzy head. He gobbled down the muffins in two gulps and slurped up most of the water. Then he gave her hand a grateful lick and trotted off into the night.

*   *   *

The next morning, Shannon opened the bedroom curtains to a magical winter wonderland. The rolling lawns, dormant flower beds, bushes, and trees all were covered with a pristine blanket of white. In the distance, the icy sea frothed and roared. The prediction for snow had been right. Her home country, Scotland, frequently had wild winter storms, but snow was a rare occurrence along the low-lying Oregon coast. However, according to Alec, the mountain ranges got tons of snow, and the twins were looking forward to going skiing during Christmas vacation.

Shannon lingered by the window for a few minutes, drinking in the peaceful scene. The first snowfall of the year was always especially beautiful with its quiet, clean transformation of the bleak autumn landscape. Then, eager to make the trek to the tree farm, she dressed in thick wool socks, flannel shirt, jeans, and boots before heading downstairs for breakfast.

Always an early riser, Deborah had already made coffee. Wearing an apron over a long-sleeved blue dress, she stood at the counter, breaking eggs into a bowl. "Good morning," she said with a smile. "How does scrambled eggs with bacon sound?"

Shannon poured a cup of coffee. "Perfect, thank you. I could use a hot breakfast on such a cold day. I'm going out to Olson's Tree Farm this morning with Betty and Kate to get trees for here and the shop." A thought struck her. "I plan to get a really big tree this year, and we'll need more ornaments. Did Victoria have any?" The small box she had brought from Scotland had sufficed for the small tree they put up last year, a less-than-perfect but fragrant fir the twins had found in the woods beyond the gardens.

Deborah laughed as she poured the eggs into a sizzling-hot frying pan. "Did she have ornaments? Oh my, yes. A hundred years' worth." She picked up a wooden spoon and began to stir the eggs.

Shannon popped bread into the toaster. "Let's look after we eat. I think we'll have time before I need to leave."

They found the ornaments easily in the sprawling attic, thanks to Deborah's excellent memory. "It's been a long time since we had a big tree," she said, leading the way to three stacked plastic tubs next to an old wooden rocking horse and a dressmaker's form with an impossibly tiny waist. "For the last few years, we just had a small one in the study, since that's where Victoria spent most of her time."

Shannon took the top tub down and peeked inside. Strings of lights and garlands, all neatly wound into bundles. She set it aside and picked up the next one. "I'm really looking forward to Christmas," she said. "In just a few days, the twins will be home. I can't wait." The second tub held ornaments and bunches of old-fashioned silver tinsel.

"I think candles and other decorations are in this box." Deborah dragged a cardboard box out of the shadows. "Will you want to have a formal Christmas dinner? Oh, we used to have some grand feasts here, I tell you."

"Absolutely." Shannon pulled open the third tub to reveal

more ornaments. It was going to be fun looking through them; the yellowed boxes looked intriguingly ancient. She gazed fondly at the housekeeper, who had a smudge of dust on her nose. "Let's make it a Christmas to remember!"

*   *   *

At the store, Shannon found the dog curled up on the back step, the only dry surface left after the snowfall. As she approached, he picked up his head and gazed at her hopefully. "You're still here? What am I going to do with you?" Reaching into his thick neck ruff, she felt around for a collar. Nothing. Close up, she noticed his fur was matted and dirty. He was obviously a stray.

She thought for a moment. Since she was on her way to Kate's, she might as well take the mutt along and get him cleaned up. Maybe Kate could keep him for a few days and try to find his owner.

While in the store, she wrote Essie a note to look for a tree stand in the storeroom, and she grabbed another muffin for the dog. *He must be starving.* Then she drove over to Ultimutt Grooming, the dog riding in the passenger seat with his head out the window.

He readily followed Shannon to the front door, which was locked. She knocked on the glass, and after a moment, Kate came out of the grooming room, wiping her arms on a towel. With a wave and a smile, she hurried to the door and unlocked it. Kate had a fondness for funny animal T-shirts, and today her choice depicted a white bull terrier sporting a black eye with "You should see the other guy" printed below. "Let me get Mrs. Thompson's poodle ready for drying, and then we can go," she said. Noticing the dog, she gave a whistle of appreciation. "Who's your friend?"

"He's a stray that's been hanging around the store. Poor thing was outside all night in the snowstorm. I thought maybe you could help me find his owner."

"I sure will. Bring him in, and we'll get him fixed up." Kate selected a bright purple collar and leash from the wall display and snapped them on, then handed Shannon the leash to hold. Crouching down, she did a quick check revealing that, yes, the dog was indeed a male and fortunately already neutered. She gave his head a thorough rub, and he showed his appreciation by licking her hands. "You're a lover, aren't you?" she said with a laugh. "Let's take him out back and give him some food and water. He can stay here for now. And when we get back from the farm, I'll give him a bath. I'm sure he'll clean up beautifully."

Behind them, the doorbell jingled, and they turned to see Hillary entering the store. She'd barely opened her mouth to greet them when the dog began to bark ferociously, straining at the leash. Hillary backed up against the front door, petrified.

"Stop it, Boyd!" Shannon commanded, jerking on the leash. To her surprise, the dog immediately quieted, sitting at her feet but continuing to watch Hillary.

"That is really odd. He seems friendly enough. Maybe you startled him," Kate said to Hillary.

"I don't understand it either," Hillary said. "I prefer cats, but I get along with most dogs. Just not that one, I guess." She slid behind the counter and signed on to the cash register. "I'll let you handle him."

Kate turned to Shannon. "Let's take him out back so Hillary can get to work."

In the grooming room, where Mrs. Thompson's poodle stood waiting patiently in the big sink, Kate pulled a can of dog food out of a cupboard "'Boyd,' huh? Looks like you gave him a name," she said as she handed the can, an opener, and a bowl to Shannon. She began to towel off the poodle.

"I suppose I did," Shannon said, opening the can and emptying it into the bowl. "It just slipped out. *Boyd* means 'yellow' in Gaelic, so it seems to suit him." Boyd nudged her leg, seemingly in agreement, before attacking the food.

*　*　*

"Slow down," Betty said. "We're almost there." Just up ahead, Shannon spotted a big wooden sign reading "Olson's Tree Farm— Christmas Year-Round" in green lettering. A red sleigh filled with small decorated Christmas trees was below it.

Shannon slowed Old Blue, the 1955 Ford pickup that was part of her inheritance, and turned into the wide dirt drive that was bordered on both sides by woods. A short distance in, the woods gave way to acres of rolling fields lined with snow-frosted evergreens ranging from tiny to majestic in size. The clouds parted and sunlight made the snow crystals sparkle and dance like lights. All three women inhaled sharply, struck by the sight.

"How gorgeous," Kate said.

"What a perfect day to come out here," Betty agreed.

The driveway ended in a wide dirt parking lot in front of a white farmhouse with a big red barn and several outbuildings.

One open shed had several stalls filled with trees ready for sale. Another at a right angle to the first held a table and chairs for checkout and piles of cut boughs and evergreen garland.

"I wonder if anyone is around." Old Blue's door creaked open as Shannon stepped out. The barn door was shut, and there didn't appear to be anyone around the sheds.

The cranberry-red front door of the farmhouse opened and a pleasantly rotund, middle-aged woman with curly gray hair stepped out onto the wide covered porch. She waved, a big smile creasing her wide face. She wore a print dress and a handmade fisherman-knit cardigan.

"That's Marge," Betty said, scrambling to the ground with a wince. Her arthritis always acted up on damp days, and the drive in the cramped pickup cab hadn't helped.

"Why, hello," Marge called when they got closer. "I know that truck!" She peered at Shannon through thick glasses. Her brown eyes were unexpectedly large and beautiful, with thick lashes. "You must be Shannon." She grasped Shannon's hand in a firm, warm grip. "You have the look of her, all right."

"I'm so happy to meet you," Shannon said. "I heard you were a good friend of my grandmother's."

"That's right. Come on in. I've just put the kettle on."

Betty introduced Kate to Marge, and the quartet made their way down a wide hallway with polished hardwood floors to the big kitchen at the back of the house. Here a kettle sang on a six-burner gas stove, and two cats, one gray and one tiger, basked in the sunshine pouring through a picture window overlooking the Christmas trees.

"Please have a seat," Marge said, indicating the scrubbed pine trestle table with eight chairs around it. In the middle was a plate heaped with what looked to be homemade cinnamon doughnuts. Marge emptied a cobalt-blue teapot into the big porcelain sink, then stuffed it with teabags. "This imported blend is one your grandmother introduced me to," she said to Shannon. "She said your mother, Beth, recommended it to her."

Shannon noticed that the mention of her mother, who had been restored to her life when she first moved to Apple Grove, didn't sting any more. Instead, she was perhaps going to get a good cup of tea, something rare in her adopted home.

"Shannon loves her tea," Betty said. "She's been trying to teach me how to make it the right way."

"Warm the teapot and boil the water," Shannon said. "That's the most important thing."

"That's what Victoria told me," Marge said, pouring steaming hot water into the teapot. Kate helped carry cups and saucers to the table, and soon they were sipping good tea and munching on doughnuts.

"The boys need a big breakfast every morning before they start work," Marge said. "I try to bake every day." She went on, "Besides Gary, we've got two young men helping us. Dick hasn't been able to do much with his broken leg, and there's a lot to do this time of year."

"I can imagine," Shannon said. "That's why we're here. To buy trees."

"And you've got some real beauties out there," Kate put in. "I usually don't put up a tree in my apartment, but I'm thinking about it now."

"What do you hear from Finn?" Betty asked. "Finn is Marge's son," she explained.

Marge's affable smile vanished. "Actually, Finn is here. He came back a couple of days ago. He's been in Asia, teaching English."

"Yes, I did hear that he was teaching overseas," Betty went on. "You must be so proud. Finn is a lovely young man," she told the others. "He looks like a younger Dick, but he has his mother's eyes."

Marge's only response to this praise was a shrug. A troubled and sad expression briefly filled her beautiful eyes, something she hid behind a sip of tea from her cup before averting her gaze out the kitchen window.

Not the reaction you'd expect from a mother happy to see her son come home, Shannon mused silently. *Something is very wrong here.*

An uncomfortable silence fell, broken only by the ticking of the regulator wall clock. After wracking her brain, Shannon gratefully thought of a different topic. "How's the new wool working out?"

Marge's face lightened. "It's beautiful! Do you want to see what I'm doing with it?"

"I'd love to," Shannon said.

Marge got up from the table with a slight groan and went to a basket beside the rocking chair next to the picture window. Shannon could picture her rocking and knitting while gazing out at the trees in all lights and seasons. Marge pulled a fuzzy blue-green bundle of knitting out of the basket and held it up with both hands, displaying the beautiful lace shawl she was making.

"Oh my," Betty said with a gasp. "That design looks like peacock feathers."

Marge beamed proudly. "That's what it's called." She brought the work over to the table so all could get a closer look.

"The baby alpaca yarn is perfect for that stitch," Shannon said.

Kate fingered the garment. "I wish I had the patience for lace knitting. It's fantastic."

"Oh, it's not that hard. I could teach you some simple stitches."

"We'd love it if you did a class at the market," Shannon said.

"Maybe I will," Marge replied. She tucked away the knitting and rejoined them at the table. "How are things going there? I've been meaning to come in, but with Dick's broken leg, it's been hard to get away."

"We've been doing really well, especially since we opened the coffee shop, Espresso Yourself. Besides Essie Engleman, the manager, I have another clerk. You must know her. Carrie Weston."

"Carrie's working for you? Oh, I'm so glad. She's had a hard time settling down to something steady."

Shannon was alarmed to hear her employee discussed in those terms, but she kept silent, hoping Marge would explain.

"She's a good girl, but she's always been rather flighty. Here, there, and everywhere. Waitress, fishing boat crew, state park attendant, lifeguard—you name it, she's done it. She and Finn are rather alike in that way, come to think of it."

"Sounds like you know her well," Betty ventured.

"I should say so. She and Finn dated all through high school, right up until he went off to college. Carrie went to the community college, but I don't think she ever settled on a degree."

Finn's old girlfriend was now dating Gary Booker, who in essence was a stand-in for Finn at the farm. Shannon wondered how the situation would go over with Finn.

"I'm hoping she and Gary will settle down," Marge continued. "I think he's good for her. He's reliable and steady. Content to stay in one place and make a life."

Unlike Finn. Maybe Gary isn't so bad after all. Shannon stood. "Marge, it's been a pleasure to meet you, but we really should get our trees and get back to town before noon. I'm sure the girls are swamped at the shop."

Kate glanced at the clock and jumped up. "And I've got a grooming appointment at one." The exuberant Kate gave Marge a hug of thank you, and after goodbyes and see-you-soons, the trio headed for the barn where Marge had said they would find Gary.

The big double door to the barn was now open, and as they approached, they heard a man say, "I don't know what you're up to, but I don't like it." Betty and Kate hung back in the drive, but Shannon moved to the doorway and looked inside.

She saw Gary Booker and a dark, sturdy man—Finn, she surmised—facing each other. Gary had his fists clenched, and Finn, wearing a work coat and jeans, was resting on a pitchfork. Next to Finn was a bale of hay he had apparently been feeding to the draft horse in a stall. As Shannon watched, Gary took a threatening step toward Finn.

4

Both men were too absorbed to notice Shannon, and as she hesitated, debating what to do, Gary sneered. "I don't take orders from you. Your dad hired me, and it's thanks to me that this place is still open. You were too busy on your world travels." This last line was delivered mockingly.

"Stay back." Finn feinted with the pitchfork and Betty gasped. She and Kate had crept up to the doorway and were now looking on with Shannon. "You don't know anything about it," Finn snarled. "They're my parents, and I know you're up to something. It smells a lot like the stuff I clean out of Roscoe's stall every morning." He spit on the floor, expressing his disgust.

As Finn got angrier, Gary relaxed, a smile creeping across his face. Shannon got the sense he enjoyed provoking the other man. In a mild, oh-so-reasonable tone, he said, "All I'm doing is what you should have done. Now it's too late." In a nonchalant display, he crossed his arms, his grin now frankly smug.

Finn's face went beet red and his neck tightened. "What do you mean by that, you—"

Finn's shouting was interrupted by Dick's booming voice. "Cut it out, both of you!" He came buzzing along in his chair from the back door of the barn. To Shannon's surprise, he glared at his son. "Did your book learning drive out all your common sense, boy? I can't have fighting on the farm, especially during business hours. Didn't you notice we have customers?" He nodded toward the women.

Finn turned and saw them watching. His face turned bright red, his embarrassment obvious. With a muttered curse, he tossed the pitchfork down on top of the hay and stalked out the back door.

"I'm sorry you had to see that," Dick grumbled in his raspy voice.

With appreciative glances at all three women, Gary said, "How may I help you ladies?" His attitude was genial and proprietary, like that of a host.

Shannon thought about leaving, as the overt conflict made her uneasy. The others felt the same, she could tell. But something told her to stay. Perhaps it was the idea of honoring her grandmother's friendship with Marge—or maybe she was just nosy. Either way, something did stink, like Finn said. And she wanted to know what it was.

Out in the fresh air, walking among the snowy rows of trees to pick out the best ones, the tension dissolved, and the friends began to enjoy the day. Shannon had worried about Betty's arthritis, but the slow stroll actually seemed to help. Kate was like a little girl as she ran from one tree to another, exclaiming, "Oh, this one's perfect. Well, maybe this one is a little better. What do you think?" At intervals, life-size wooden snowman signs set in the wide main aisle informed visitors of tree species and the route back to the barn. Someone—no doubt Marge—had decorated them with red wool hats and scarves for the season.

"What size tree are you looking for?" Gary asked Shannon.

"I'm thinking fifteen feet for the house," she said. "We have a two-story entryway."

He whistled. "Nice. You'll want a noble fir, then. Those are our biggest trees." He pointed to a line of enormous trees in the distance.

"How many types of trees do you have?" Betty asked, curious.

"A bunch," Gary replied. "Let's see. We have Douglas fir, Fraser fir, the noble fir I mentioned, blue spruce, and Scotch pine."

"So many to choose from," Betty murmured.

"Folks like the variety," Gary said. "And some like cutting their own. A lot of families make a tradition of coming back every year for our Christmas on the Farm event. It's this Saturday, actually. We have hayrides, music, hot chocolate, and Marge's cookies and doughnuts. Maybe even a visit from Santa Claus." He winked. "Santa might have a broken leg this year, though."

Creating a new family tradition was appealing, and the twins would be home in time for the event, Shannon realized with a leap of her heart. Tomorrow, actually. She could hardly wait to see them again, although they had just been home for Thanksgiving. "I'm going to wait on buying the tree for the house," she said. "I'll bring the twins out this weekend and let them pick one out."

"What fun," Betty said. "We used to do that with our kids."

"What kind of tree should I get?" Kate asked. "I live in an apartment and I don't have many decorations."

Grinning, Gary took her arm. "Right this way, young lady. I've got some baby Frasers that are just right."

Betty watched, amazed, as Gary and Kate went off, laughing and chatting like old friends.

"That's the famous Gary Booker charm in action," Shannon said dryly.

"So I see! I guess we're on our own for a few minutes. Help me pick one out." Betty pulled a nearby branch toward her nose and inhaled deeply, then shared it with Shannon. "I think I like these Fraser firs the best. They smell great."

"The smell of Christmas," Shannon agreed.

In the end, Shannon chose a six-foot noble fir for the shop. The arrangement of the branches gave more room for decorations, and that's what Shannon wanted in order to display shop wares and ornaments made by the loft artists. Betty selected an eight-foot Fraser fir for the inn parlor, and Kate bought a baby Fraser for her apartment. Shannon also ordered cut greens for the wreath-making class.

To her surprise, Chaz Loper emerged from one of the sheds to help Gary load the trees in the back of Old Blue. He had dated Lara briefly. "Hi, Mrs. McClain," he said shyly.

"Hi, Chaz. How do you like working here?" Shannon was glad to see that he was gainfully employed after a difficult period of juvenile delinquency.

"It's great," he said, smiling. "How is Lara—?"

"Come on, Chaz, we don't have all day," Gary snapped.

"I enjoy it most of the time," Chaz added in a whisper. With a rueful grimace, he trotted over to help Gary push one of the trees through the binder.

While waiting, Shannon and the others explored the farm on the opposite side of the parking lot. Here they came across a big pond surrounded by white geese and ducks. A coating of ice had formed, and the fowl were loudly proclaiming their displeasure with honks and quacks. Some waddled back and forth on the ice, hunting in vain for a patch of open water.

As the women stood laughing at the sight, Finn approached through the trees. "Hey, Mrs. Russo," he said to Betty, nodding at the others. Under his orange knit cap, his face was glum.

"Call me Betty," she said. "We're all adults here." She introduced Shannon and Kate.

"I guess I wasn't too adult earlier. I'm sorry about the scene in the barn. It was really embarrassing to have you see that."

"Don't worry about it," Betty said kindly. "All families have arguments. And many parents and children don't always see eye to eye."

"I suppose. Our situation is a little worse than that. We've got an outsider sticking his big nose in." Finn picked up a stick and threw it at the pond. Hitting the ice, it skittered along and startled a goose, which flapped its wings vigorously.

"Are all these geese and ducks pets?" Kate asked.

"No," Finn said. "We raise them for market. They're actually shipped all over the country."

"People eat geese?" Kate made a face.

"They're much tastier than turkey," Finn assured her.

Shannon felt a twinge of excitement. She wanted to make Christmas dinner really special, and how better than to serve a traditional Scottish goose as the main dish? "I'd like to order one," she said. She thought about the guest list. "Make that two."

"I'll tell Dad to reserve two for you."

"Thanks, Finn." In accord, the group began to walk back to the parking lot, Shannon and Kate ahead, Finn and

Betty trailing behind. Although she wasn't trying to eavesdrop, Shannon could clearly hear Finn tell Betty, "I'm really worried about Mom and Dad. Not only is Gary taking over the tree business, he's convinced them to subdivide and sell house lots on the land near the main road. They already paid for a surveyor. I found the plans in the office."

"Maybe that would be a good business move," Betty said cautiously. "Bring in some cash for a cushion."

"The thing is, Dad has always been firmly opposed to developing the land. It's been in our family for over one hundred years, and every acre is precious to him. I think Gary is pressuring them, but the problem is proving it."

He didn't mention Gary being a signer on the bank accounts, and Shannon wondered what would happen once he found out.

*   *   *

"I love my tree, but that was a pretty intense scene at the farm," Kate commented as they pulled out of the farm road. The snow on the main road had melted and the tar was a glistening black. Old Blue's tires splashed through occasional deep puddles.

"I was sorry to see Dick still being so hard on Finn," Betty said. "They've never really gotten along that well. Finn's more like his mother, interested in books and languages, and that disappointed Dick. He wanted him to take over the farm, but Finn just wasn't interested. Of course, that's happening in many farming families. The younger generation moves away."

Shannon thought about her twins. Alec was quiet—though mischievous enough—and a science student. In contrast, Lara was creative, outgoing, and working toward a business career. She loved to sing and perform; Alec would rather die than do that, she was sure. "You have to let kids be themselves," she said. "There's no point in forcing them into a mold."

"So true," Betty replied. "My three are all different."

They passed two pickup trucks parked beside the road, one white and one green. Three men in hunter-orange vests and hats and carrying crossbows were heading into the woods.

"What are they doing?" Shannon asked.

Betty craned her neck to look back. "I thought I recognized the white truck. They're turkey hunters staying with us. The land next to the farm is a designated public hunting area."

"There's an option, Shannon," Kate joked. "You could shoot a turkey for Christmas dinner."

"No thanks. We'd all starve since I couldn't hit the broad side of a barn with an arrow."

"Neither could I," Kate replied. "You have to be quite strong, I understand." Silent for a moment, she said, "I thought it was odd the way Gary acted like it was his farm."

"I noticed," Betty said. "No wonder Finn is upset."

"You were right about Gary being a flirt, Shannon," Kate added. "My goodness. He almost swept me off my feet. I had to remind myself that he's dating Carrie."

"He is good-looking," Betty said slyly. "But so is Finn."

Kate shrugged. "Yeah, I guess." She studied the passing woods and fields. "He's not my type. I'm beginning to wonder if anyone out there is."

5

Later that afternoon, Shannon and Carrie were behind the counter of Espresso Yourself, dreaming up hot chocolate drinks for the coffee shop's menu. Outside the window, the blue dusk of winter was falling, and the gas streetlamps cast a cheerful glow on passersby. Essie had found a stand for the tree, and it stood in a corner, waiting to be decorated.

It had been another busy day, and Shannon was glad it was finally winding down. Tomorrow she was planning to pick up the twins at college, and she wanted to get just a few more things done before she left for the evening.

"We definitely need one with peppermint," Carrie said. "We can call it the Candy Cane." She pulled a bottle of peppermint syrup from the row beside the espresso machine and placed it on the counter. "I want to try one right now."

"I like that," Shannon said. "And we'll call the white-chocolate drink the Snowman." She wrote both names on the new chalkboard she'd bought for this purpose. "It will have lots of whipped cream. White on white."

Carrie laughed. "I have an idea. How about a double chocolate called the Naughty? And the milk chocolate flavor can be the Nice."

"Cute! I'll put them side by side. Naughty or Nice." Shannon added them to the list. "What can we call hot chocolate with coffee? We should have one. Everyone loves mocha."

"The Rudolph?" Carrie suggested. "Since the caffeine makes you fly?"

Shannon and Carrie burst out laughing. The doorbell jingled and Shannon looked up. Her heart started thumping when she recognized two tall and familiar figures, even as bundled up as they were in thick coats and hats.

Alec and Lara! She rushed from behind the counter, meeting them in the shop doorway. Reaching out both arms, she gathered them into a three-way hug. "Och, I'm so glad to see you both!" She felt tears spring into her eyes but quickly blinked them away.

"Hi, Mum," Alec said. "It's good to be home."

"We got a ride," Lara said after giving her mother a loud kiss on the cheek. "We thought we'd surprise you."

"You sure did. And what a good surprise."

"You're open until seven tonight, right?" Alec asked. "We thought we would hang out with you until then. We already left our stuff at home. Deborah said to tell you she's making homemade chicken potpie for dinner."

"My favorite," Lara said, beaming. Turning to Carrie, she asked, "What are you doing?"

"Making hot chocolate drinks. You want one?" Carrie pointed to the chalkboard. "Pick from that list."

The twins studied the chalkboard. "I'm definitely having the Naughty," Lara said. "Double chocolate ... yum!"

"Do you have one with coffee?" Alec asked. He yawned. "I've been staying up late, studying for exams. I am so wiped."

Shannon and Carrie exchanged amused looks. "We can make that," Shannon said. "We were just talking about what to call it."

Alec yawned again. "How about Jingle Beans?"

"Perfect. One Jingle Beans and one Naughty coming right up."

Lara gave her mother another hug. "I'm so excited about Christmas!" she exclaimed. "The town looks so pretty. And it snowed last night!"

"I am too," Shannon said. "I even ordered goose for Christmas dinner."

"Roast goose," Alec said. "Awesome."

"Mum," Lara said hesitantly. "Do you think ... can we ask Beth to come for Christmas?"

"Of course! She's part of the family."

The twins exchanged glances, smiling. With a flourish, Carrie delivered their drinks, piled high with whipped cream and topped with a dusting of chocolate.

"Is there anything we can do for you, Mum?" Alec asked after making great inroads into his cocoa.

"How about decorating the tree for me? I have some ornament kits we made up. And handmade ornaments from the artists." Shannon pointed to the boxes waiting by the tree.

"I'd love to," Lara said. "Are we getting a tree for the house?"

"I thought we'd go out to Olson's Tree Farm this Saturday and cut our own. Not that I didn't like the one you found last year at the mansion," she added quickly, "but I want a really tall one for the entryway, and Olson's has them."

"It *was* kind of homely," Lara said, laughing.

"Sounds good," Alec said, pulling a string of lights out of a box. "As you know, I like chopping things down."

The door jingled again and a young, good-looking man with a neat beard entered the coffee shop. "Howdy, folks," he said with a nod of greeting. He unbuttoned his wool coat and hung it on the back of a chair.

Shannon looked up from pricing the box of handblown globes one of the artists had made, which were destined for the tree. The man looked familiar. Where had she seen him?

He sensed her looking at him and smiled. "I'm Jake Stager," he said. "Reporter for *The Oregonian*."

"That's right," Shannon said. He'd been pretty pushy while reporting on the murder of Fredo Benson, an artist who had rented a loft. "No murders here today, Mr. Stager," she said lightly.

"I guess I deserve that," he said with a sheepish grin. Turning to Carrie, who was waiting for his order, he said, "I'd like the Jingle Beans, please. Got a long ride home tonight."

"Coming right up."

Shannon relented and asked, "Are you here on a story? Maybe I can help."

He looked around at the shop's craft displays, decorations, and the tree Alec and Lara were decorating. "Actually, you might be able to. I'm doing a feature on Christmas in Oregon's quaintest town, and this year, Apple Grove is it. I'd like to include your business as one of the destinations."

"Thank you. I'd appreciate that."

Carrie leaned on the counter with both arms and began to fill Jake in on Christmas events he might want to cover. A couple of middle-aged women entered the craft store, and Shannon went to wait on them. They purchased several of the Christmas stocking kits as well as some yarn. Chattering about how happy their grandchildren would be with the stockings, they pushed through the front door just as Kate entered. With her was a clean and fluffy Boyd, who immediately pulled against the leash toward Shannon.

"Doesn't he look great?" Kate said. "I was taking him for a walk, and I thought I'd bring him by to see his rescuer."

Shannon patted the dog's soft fur. "You look so much better, don't you, Boyd?"

Big brown eyes fixed on her face, and he panted as though laughing in agreement. Noticing the dog, Lara and Alec came out to fuss over him. Kate told them the story of how Shannon had found him sleeping outside the shop.

"You should keep him, Mum," Lara said, crouching down and ruffling the dog's thick neck fur. "You're a good boy," she assured him. She was rewarded by a kiss on the cheek from his wet nose.

"She even named him," Kate said mischievously. "Boyd."

"'Yellow' in Gaelic," Alec said. "Good choice."

Shannon demurred about keeping the dog, but she offered to watch him while Kate had a hot chocolate since dogs weren't allowed in the coffee shop. With a groan, the dog flopped down on the wooden floor beside her and was soon asleep.

Shannon's next task was to inventory the jewelry case. The silver Madonna and Child Christmas pendants decorated with blue and gold enamel were almost gone, she was happy to note. She'd have to schedule time to make more.

After finishing the inventory so she could order more from Essie and the other artists, Shannon leaned her head into the coffee shop. "If you want to go home early, that would be fine, Carrie. With the twins here, we can handle things."

"Really?" Carrie's eyes lit up. "I have a date with Gary. Let me give him a buzz." Walking out from behind the counter, she pulled out her cellphone.

Kate was sitting beside Jake at the counter, and from what Shannon overheard, they and the twins were discussing skiing. "I'd be happy to take you guys," Jake said. "I've skied all the mountains, and I know where to find the deepest powder. And the best après-ski events too."

"That would be awesome," Alec said.

"Make it a Sunday, and I can go," Kate said, smiling at Jake. He smiled back. "For sure."

Looks like someone has a new friend!

Frowning, Carrie flipped her phone closed. "I can't reach him." Following Shannon into the craft shop, she said, "Gary is supposed to meet me here at seven. If I don't reach him and he shows up here, can you tell him I went home?"

"Of course."

Kate and Jake were next to leave, and the duo were so busy chatting that they barely said goodbye to Shannon while collecting Boyd and heading out the door. Soon after, the twins helped Shannon close up, all of them looking forward to going home to Deborah's delicious meal.

Just before they left, the store phone rang. It was Carrie. "Have you seen Gary?" she asked.

"No, I haven't." Glancing at the clock, Shannon saw it was seven fifteen.

"OK. Have a good night." Carrie's voice was choked, like she was holding back tears.

Shannon had a sinking feeling that, thanks to Gary Booker, more trouble was on the horizon.

6

Carrie seemed fine the next day, so Shannon didn't ask her about what had happened with Gary. It was probably safer to assume that everything was all right rather than risk upsetting her.

From the moment the doors opened at ten, they were again happily inundated with customers seeking craft supplies and gifts. During a late-afternoon lull, Shannon was finally able to break away and make calls to suppliers for reorders of the most popular merchandise. Fortunately, several still had stock on hand. She was calling the last vendor when she looked up to see a tall hunk of a man easily leaning in the doorway, his piercing blue eyes riveted on her. Michael Stone.

She quickly hung up the phone, feeling a big smile stretch across her face. "Hey, stranger," she said. "How have you been?"

Michael, co-owner of Stone & McCrary, an international security consultation firm, had been out of town for almost a week. Although she had been busier than ever, she'd missed him. Just how much was apparent in the joy she felt upon seeing his face.

"I just got back this afternoon." He looked at his expensive, high-tech watch. Everything Michael owned was expensive and high-tech. "About fifteen minutes ago."

She pushed the paperwork to one side. "So I'm your first stop?" she asked slyly.

"Maybe." His nonchalant voice belied the grin that told her he was very glad to see her too. "And unfortunately, I can't stay long," he added with a grimace. "I've got a conference call with another client. I was hoping to take you out to dinner, but now I'll have to take a rain check."

"I guess business is booming," she said lightly, hiding her disappointment. "That's a good thing, right? We're busy too. Our Christmas season has been fantastic so far."

"That's great. The shop looks really good, all decorated."

"Thanks. And when you have a chance, you have to try the fancy Christmas drinks we added to the coffee shop menu."

"I'll do that. Are the twins home yet? You must be excited."

"Yes, they are. They came home early and surprised me last night." She had a thought. "Saturday we're going out to Olson's to cut a tree. Apparently they're having music and other festivities that day. Do you want to come along?" She held her breath, not sure a sophisticated man like Michael would want to do something so ordinary as tramp through fields to pick out a Christmas tree.

To her relief, he nodded and said, "I'd love to. I used to do that when I was a kid. My dad and I would go out in our woods and find a tree. They weren't as pretty as the tree-farm ones, but I thought they were perfect anyway."

They made arrangements to meet at the farm, and Shannon turned back to her work. She needed to get things wrapped up so she could get ready for the wreath-making class. A dozen women, including all the Purls except Betty, had signed up.

Kate and Hillary arrived early and set up the folding tables the students would use as workstations. Today Hillary was a little more animated, Shannon noticed, even smiling as she directed the classroom layout. Shannon laid out a wreath form—double circular rings of metal—and clippers and wire in each place. On a separate table, she put spools of velvet and silk ribbon, jingle bells, fake fruit, and tiny Christmas balls. Behind the counter, Essie prepared the cups and plates for the hot chocolate and sugar cookies the class would enjoy. Melanie arrived next, carrying a box holding berries in various colors, pinecones, and interesting dried plants and flowers from The Flower Pot. She arranged them beside the other decorations.

"This is awesome," Hillary said, appearing at Shannon's elbow as she organized the ornaments. "What a great variety of stuff to choose from. Now we just need the greenery."

Shannon glanced at the clock behind the counter. "They should be here any minute." Peering through the window and out into the street, she saw a green pickup truck back into a parking space in front of the store. The driver-side door opened and Gary emerged from the truck. "There's Gary now."

Making a couple of trips, Gary brought in bundles of fragrant evergreen branches tied with twine and set them in a row next to the trim table. Today he wore a leather jacket and pressed jeans instead of work clothes, but a cut, swollen lip marred his otherwise handsome face. Shannon wondered where that had come from.

Gary pointed to each one in turn, informing Shannon of their species. "Noble fir, Doug fir, cedar, and juniper. You should get a good mix out of that. More attractive than just one type of evergreen." He bent and sliced the twine on each bundle with his jackknife.

Shannon looked around for Hillary, who really should have been the one inspecting the delivery. How strange. She was nowhere in sight. "Did you see where Hillary went?" she called to Essie.

Essie shook her head. Melanie and Kate hadn't seen her either. Carrie was in the craft store cashing out a customer, and Shannon didn't want to interrupt. Shrugging, she turned back to Gary.

"These will work," he assured her. "I've made wreaths before." He pulled a branch out of the bag. "You cut each one into smaller pieces, the way you want them. We packed enough for about fifteen wreaths, like you said."

"I guess I'll take your word for it. What do I owe you?"

Gary reached into his pocket and pulled out two pieces of paper. "One is the invoice for the greens; the other the confirmation of your goose order. Marge said you can pay for both when you pick up the birds."

Her shift over, Carrie sashayed up, dressed in an overcoat and clutching her handbag. "Hi, Gary," she cooed. Her smile turned to concern when she noticed his cut lip. "Ooh! What happened?" She extended delicate fingers toward his face.

He pulled back, wincing. "Finn and I got into it. No big deal."

Again? Shannon wanted to add, but she refrained.

"Finn's back?" Carrie asked, her eyes wide.

"Yep. And he's been nothing but trouble. Dick and Marge better do something about it. We can't go on like this." He shook his head. "Well, never mind *him*. Are you ready to go? I'm starving." His grin was charming, despite the injury. "I'm going to take you somewhere really nice to make up for canceling last night. Even though it wasn't my fault."

"That sounds wonderful." Carrie took his arm, her good humor restored. "How about The Apple Grove Inn? They have a fantastic menu."

With that, they left, but on the way out, Gary made a point of greeting both Kate and Essie. The stiff set of Carrie's shoulders revealed she had noticed and was not pleased.

The rest of the class attendees, including Joyce, had arrived by the time Hillary came back into the coffee shop. Talking at full volume, they were milling around, drinking hot chocolate, and picking out trim materials with exclamations of delight.

"Where have you been?" Shannon asked Hillary. "I was worried about you." *And worried we'd have a class without an instructor!*

Hillary rubbed her stomach, making a face. "I guess my dinner didn't agree with me. I had to take a quick trip to the restroom. Sorry about that." Her gaze fell on the bundles of greens and she quickly examined each one. "Perfect. Let's distribute some of each type to each student. We're making a really unusual and beautiful mixed evergreen wreath."

Soon each class member had a pile of greens in front of her along with her selected trims and ribbon. Hillary led them through the process of cutting the branches into smaller sprigs, bundling ten sprigs together with wire, and wiring the bundles onto the frames. Her method was fast and easy, and soon everyone had a thick, attractive wreath made up of evergreens that varied nicely in color and shape. The next step was tying big ribbon bows under Hillary's tutelage.

"She really knows what's she's doing," Melanie commented to Shannon. They were side by side at a table with Kate. "Maybe she can make wreaths for The Flower Pot."

"That would probably suit her better," Kate whispered to Shannon, "since she's not so great with dogs."

"That's true." Shannon had to admit Hillary was an odd bundle of contradictions.

The class moved on to trimming the wreaths, and soon they each had a gorgeous creation that reflected their individual tastes and decorating styles. Shannon chose a red bow and fruit and gold ball trimmings to set off Paisley Mansion's tan stucco exterior and Mediterranean style. Joyce used pink ribbon and berries, of course, and trimmed her wreath with black and white balls. Kate's was traditional with pinecones, berries, and red ribbon; Melanie's was an ethereal confection of dried plants, white berries, and a striped bow. Soon after, the class broke up, but the Purls and Hillary stayed to clean up, chat, and indulge in celebratory refreshments. The class had gone extremely well, all agreed.

"Another sugar cookie, Joyce?" Shannon asked, passing around the tray.

"One unfortunate thing about this time of year," Joyce said with a groan, "is all the good food. I have to work hard to maintain my weight." Relenting, she took one cookie. A small one. "But I can't complain, since people do order a lot from the bakery for Christmas. They've finally realized it's OK to have someone else bake pies. I've already got a list of orders as long as your arm."

"Do you make mince pies?" Shannon asked. "They're traditional in Scotland."

"What's in a mince pie?" Kate asked.

"Apples, raisins, candied fruit, and spices," Shannon explained. "Of course, the old recipes used ground venison or beef, hence the full name of 'mincemeat.'"

"Ugh," Melanie said with a shudder. "Venison pie. I'm glad they leave that ingredient out nowadays."

"You know I'm always looking for new recipes," Joyce said. "I'd love to try mince. Maybe even make mince tarts too. A lot of people like tarts and mini-pies."

"I'll get you the recipe and you can make me one," Shannon said. "This year I'm doing a Scottish feast for Christmas."

"Yeah, she's actually having goose!" Kate put in. "I never knew people ate them."

"Goose is good," Hillary said quietly. She'd been sitting with her hot chocolate, not saying much. With the voluble Purls, Shannon couldn't blame her.

"Gosh, a big Christmas feast sounds wonderful, even with goose," Kate said wistfully. "I'm not visiting my parents in Florida this year, so I'll probably make do with a turkey TV dinner."

"Oh no, we can't have that," Shannon said. "You must join us for dinner."

Kate blushed. "I didn't say that so you'd feel sorry for me."

"No, I insist. And you too, Hillary—if you're not doing anything, please come."

"Thanks. I don't have any family or anyplace to go." Her tone was bitter and self-pitying. "It's just me against the world."

Disconcerted, the Purls exchanged glances.

"Don't feel that way," Joyce said kindly. "You're among friends here."

Hillary ducked her head, studying her cocoa as if it held all the answers.

What on earth is her story? Shannon again wondered.

Later, Shannon headed home in Old Blue, tired but grateful after another successful day. As she turned into Larkspur Lane, snowflakes began to fall, spinning and dancing in the headlights. She laughed out loud. Snow again? The weather forecasters were right. It was going to be a banner year for snow. The twirling flakes reminded her of the multitude of blessings that had befallen her since she had first moved to the States. Everything in her life was just about perfect.

Entering the Paisley mansion driveway, she drove slowly along the winding curves, enjoying the beauty of the snow-covered landscape. As she approached the sprawling house, dark except for an entrance light, she caught her breath in awe.

In each of the front windows, an electric candle shone, casting a warm glow that said "Welcome home." The twins must have put them up that afternoon.

Home. The contentment she felt let her know that yes, she was indeed home. Scotland would always hold a special place in her heart, but Apple Grove had become her home.

She parked the truck in the garage, but before getting out, she dug her cellphone out of her purse. She needed to make a certain call right now.

The phone rang and rang and she felt a pang of insecurity. Maybe it was too late, and she should try again tomorrow. Her finger hovered over the End icon.

Just then, the ringing stopped. "Hello? Shannon?" Beth

sounded both hopeful and nervous. Despite the great strides Shannon and Beth had made in their relationship, at times there was still a little uneasiness between them.

"Hi, Beth. I hope it's not too late to call."

"No no, that's fine, dear. Is everyone all right?"

"Yes, we are. I was wondering if you would come here for Christmas."

Beth gasped. "Oh, I'd love to! Thanks for asking me."

"Great! The twins will be so happy. And so will I. If you come on Christmas Eve, you can stay overnight and go to church with us. And then we'll have a big feast on Christmas Day."

7

Shannon took another sip of coffee and gazed out at the snowy landscape. Today they were going out to the tree farm, and the twins were upstairs getting ready. The weather was predicted to stay unseasonably cold, which meant that with luck, the snow cover might last.

Deborah bustled up to the table and began to clear the remains of a hearty vegetable omelet-and-bacon breakfast.

"Leave it," Shannon said. "I'll help you in a minute. I want to talk to you about Christmas dinner."

Deborah refilled her coffee cup and sat down. "I'm really looking forward to cooking for everyone. What are you thinking for the menu?"

"I want to go as traditional as possible. So besides the chestnut-stuffed goose, I want a real Christmas plum pudding."

"Ooh, there's a challenge. I've never made one."

"Neither have I," Shannon admitted. "I know you have to steam it for hours."

"Well, leave it to me, dear. I'll find a recipe and figure it out."

The twins came clattering into the kitchen. "Ready, Mum?" Alec asked.

"I can't wait to get our tree," Lara said, beaming.

Shannon drained her cup and stood up. "Let's help Deborah clean up, and then we can get on the road."

*   *   *

In contrast to earlier in the week, the parking lot at the farm was full, and Shannon had to squeeze Old Blue between a minivan and a huge SUV. Throngs of people, mostly families with small children, were milling around the farmyard between the barns and sheds. The draft horse, hitched up to a hay wagon, stood waiting for the order to pull his burden of passengers. Jake Stager, the reporter, was taking a picture of the horse for his article. In one of the sheds, a bluegrass band featuring a banjo, fiddle, and standing bass energetically played "Jingle Bells."

"This looks fun," Lara said as the three climbed out.

"I hope I can find Michael." Shannon scanned the crowd as they walked across the drive.

"There he is." Alec pointed to a tall approaching figure in a navy blue winter parka. Spotting them, Michael waved and walked faster, edging past a family loading a Christmas tree onto the roof of their small sedan. The tree was longer than the car.

"You found us!" Shannon couldn't help but notice her quickening pulse.

Michael laughed. "Old Blue is as good as a sign in the sky. Can't miss that truck."

Shannon nudged Lara. "See? Old Blue is good for something." Lara, along with Shannon, sometimes suffered from Old Blue's temperament. For Alec, however, the '55 Ford purred like a happy kitten.

In front of the shed displaying cut trees, Marge and Dick Olson sat at a table, collecting money. Behind them was a table holding urns of hot chocolate and coffee and plates of baked goods. Dick wore a Santa hat tilted jauntily to one side.

"I want you to meet the Olsons," Shannon said. "They were my grandmother's friends." As they walked toward the shed, they passed a young man sending trees through the binder. As each tree went through the circular metal funnel, the branches were bound with netting, making the tree easier to transport.

"Hey, Chaz," Lara said to the young man. "Mum told me you were working here. How is it?"

"It's great," Chaz replied. "They even give me room and board. I love working with the trees." His grin was wide and genuine. "How's it going at college?"

Lara gave him an update before the group moved on to greet the Olsons.

Marge Olson's eyes lit up when she spotted Lara and Alec. "Victoria's great-grandchildren. How wonderful. You both remind me of her." When told they were here to cut their own tree, she pointed to a wooden box. "Saws are in that box. Have fun! And don't forget to enjoy the cocoa and cookies when you come back with that perfect tree."

Despite her cheerful tone and demeanor, Marge looked tired, almost haggard. Shannon felt a rush of sympathy for the woman. No doubt the situation with Gary and Finn was wearing on her. Shannon looked around for Finn but didn't see him. Maybe he had left for good after the last fight with Gary.

While Michael and Alec looked over the saws, Shannon heard Dick call to Chaz, "Where's Gary? It's time for the hayride."

"I don't know, boss," Chaz called back. "I haven't seen him for about an hour. I think he's out in the fields somewhere."

Dick sighed, gesturing at his broken leg with frustration. "And I can't do it with this darn leg. Get Tim to run the baler. It's too bad, but you'll have to take the horse out for the hayride." His eyes twinkled at Chaz's whoop of glee.

Alec and Michael walked up, Michael carrying a small bucksaw. "Which way?" Alec asked, gazing around at the lines of trees fanning out in every direction.

Shannon pointed to the line of the tallest trees in the distance. "I want a fifteen-footer, so we need to go out there."

"Wow, Mum," Lara exclaimed. "We've never had one that tall."

Michael whistled. "That is a big tree."

"It's for the entryway—it has to be big."

The route to the tall line of noble firs took them past the duck pond. Today there was a little open water, and the ducks and geese were swimming as well as swarming around the shore.

"I heard we're having goose for Christmas dinner," Alec said. "Which one is ours?"

Shannon pretended to think it over. "We're getting two. So that one." She pointed to a particularly fat specimen regally circling the pond. "And that one over there." Number Two was busy chasing a duck away from a morsel he had found on the ground.

"What should we call them—Gussy and Golly?"

Alec's reference to the two geese in the movie version of *Charlotte's Web* horrified Lara. "No way!" she cried. "If we give them names, I'll never be able to eat them." She snatched Alec's wool hat and ran off through the trees.

Alec followed, shouting, "I know—let's call them Lunch and Dinner!"

Lara screamed something in response.

Shannon and Michael strolled along behind them, their boots making imprints in the fresh snow. The crisp, fresh air made Shannon's nose and cheeks tingle, and she was thankful she'd worn wool socks and gloves to keep her toes and hands toasty.

"Goose? Really?" Michael's blue eyes were amused.

"It's great. Much better than turkey. You'll see."

"Oh, am I invited?" He raised a brow.

Shannon blushed. She had been planning to invite him, but properly, not like this. Finally she said, "I'm sure you're busy on Christmas Day, but if not, please do join us." She stared straight ahead, not wanting to see his expression. *Please say yes.*

Michael took her hand. "Shannon, look at me." When she turned her head, he said, "I would love to have Christmas dinner with you and your family. Thank you for including me."

"I'm so glad." Shannon's heart was singing, even as she tried to keep her voice steady. "Now let's find our tree."

The twins were still exploring when Shannon and Michael reached the far border of the property, marked by a four-foot wire fence. On the other side were open woods; on the farm side, a mowed strip with occasional hardwood trees.

"What do you think of this one?" she asked Michael. Both of them looked up to the pointed top of the tree on the end of the row, evaluating its shape and branch arrange-ment. Shannon stepped around the tree to check the back of it. A short distance away, next to a large maple, a flash of orange caught her eye. Squinting, trying to figure out what it was, she thought she saw the outline of a shoulder, like someone was sitting against the tree with his back to her. Why would someone sit on the cold, snowy ground?

Acting on impulse, she ran toward the tree.

"Where are you going?" Michael called out as he raced to catch up.

As Shannon drew closer, she saw a leg ending in a work boot stretched along the ground. The orange she had seen was a wool cap, like the hunters—and Finn—had worn.

Her heart pounded. Something was wrong. She just knew it. Panting with dread, her boots sliding in the wet snow, she reached the figure.

It took a moment for the details to sink in.

A man in work coat and pants sat slumped against the tree, his head bowed forward. An arrow protruded from the left side of his chest.

Gary Booker had been shot through the heart with an arrow.

8

It took all of Shannon's willpower not to scream, her natural inclination overruled by concern for the twins. Somehow she had to prevent them from seeing the disturbing sight of Gary, brutally slain. She still regretted allowing Alec to go into a murdered artist's apartment. Of course, she hadn't known he would stumble upon the gruesome sight—one that still haunted him at times, she was sure.

The way she knew Gary's death would haunt her.

"Shannon?" Michael emerged from the line of firs.

She waved him over. "Michael. Come. Come quickly."

The expression on his face turned serious, no doubt mirroring her own, and he jogged through the snow to her side. "Oh my," he said, his blue eyes widening. "What do we have here?" Crouching, he gently pressed Gary's carotid artery. He shook his head. "He's gone."

"That's what I thought," Shannon said. "He just seemed … so lifeless." Tears sprang to her eyes and she put her glove over her mouth, trying to hold back a sob. This wasn't the first corpse she had seen, but it was always a shock.

Michael drew Shannon into an embrace and she nestled close, comforted by his warm arms as she rested against his broad chest. He smelled so good, clean and masculine with just a hint of the minty soap he used. If only she could just stay in his arms forever, safe and protected from harm.

"Are you going to be OK?" he asked.

Nodding, she pulled back, putting her fear and shock aside with an effort. As the first witness on the scene, it was time to use her brain and log her observations.

"What do you suppose happened?" Michael asked, his hawk-like gaze sweeping up and down the fence line.

Shannon pointed to the woods beyond the fence. "People hunt over there. I saw three men going in turkey hunting just the other day. They were carrying bows."

"So perhaps it was an accident. A stray arrow." Michael pulled out his cellphone. "I'll call Chief Grayson. He's going to need to investigate."

Careful not to add too many tracks to the trampled footprints she and Michael had made in the snow next to the body, Shannon studied the ground. She could plainly see the deep prints of a large work boot along the fence line, from the same direction she had come. They ended at the maple, so they were most likely Gary's. She jumped two big steps over to the fence and peered through the square mesh. The snow on that side was an unbroken expanse of white. No prints of any kind, animal or human. Perhaps the arrow had been shot from deep in the property. Surely the farther away it was released, the greater the likelihood it was an accident. Gary was wearing orange, after all, and it would have been hard to mistake him for a turkey if he had been within view.

The shout of familiar voices warned Shannon that the twins were arriving.

"Did you find a tree?" Alec called, bursting out of the row of trees near the fir she had indeed selected. He stopped short upon spotting Shannon and Michael, and

Lara, right behind him, had to halt her progress by grabbing his shoulders.

Shannon ran toward them, careful to stay far away from Gary's prints, holding up a hand in warning. "Stay there. There's been an ... accident."

"Can't we help?" Lara asked, craning her neck to see better.

Alec's face went white. "No, Lara. Someone is dead. Right, Mum?"

"Yes," Shannon said, taking their arms and pulling them along with her.

Lara gasped. "Who is it?"

"You don't know him. He works—er, worked—here at the farm."

"That Gary they were looking for?" Alec didn't miss a thing. Shannon nodded tersely.

"How did he die?" Lara was now as pale as Alec.

"Please don't worry about it," Shannon urged. "I want you two to go home. I'm so sorry about our day being ruined."

"Me too. I was having so much fun," Lara said.

"It could be worse," Alec noted. "It could be one of *us* lying there dead. Now *that's* a day wrecker." He didn't quite pull off the jaunty, flippant tone he was attempting.

Shannon shuddered. What if one of the four of them had been hit by that stray arrow? That didn't bear thinking about.

The twins were heading down the drive in Old Blue when Chief Jack Grayson arrived in a patrol car driven by Officer Brownley. Shannon planned to get a ride home with Michael later, after they had been released from the scene. Standing at the edge of the parking lot, she flagged the chief down with a wave, and the cruiser pulled to a stop. Behind them, the farm festivities went on, the arrival of the police not setting off any alarms yet. The local force often monitored crowd activities as an essential part of their community presence.

Grayson rolled down his window. "I understand you and Michael came across a fatality, Shannon." He didn't follow up that statement with a sarcastic remark about her propensity for stumbling upon crime and murder, as he might have in the past. They had come a long way since the first few cases Shannon had found herself embroiled in—quite by accident, of course. It had taken a while to convince him that she wasn't intentionally meddling in police business.

She told him how she had discovered Gary's body and where he was located in relation to the parking lot. She explained that she and Michael were the only ones besides the police who knew about the death so far. And the twins—but she'd explain that later, she told herself.

"Sounds like a hunting accident," Grayson pronounced. "But I suppose we'd better question everyone here, see if they saw anything. We need to track Booker's movements and pin down a time of death."

Brownley whistled, looking at the full parking lot. "We've got our work cut out for us, Chief," he commented. A car with a tree tied on top passed by, the occupants staring at the police cruiser.

"I think you'd better go guard the gate," Grayson said. "Question everyone who leaves and get their names and contact information. And don't let anyone else in. It's too bad, but we're going to have to shut the farm down for the day." Grayson paused a moment, considering the size of the task, then added, "Call Doan for backup. Actually, call everyone in. We'll need a couple of officers to sweep the fields and corral everyone so they can get out of here. I'm going to talk to the Olsons. The coroner should be here any minute, and then I'll head out to the body."

Shannon stepped back as he opened the car door, relieved that it wasn't up to her to break the news to Dick and Marge.

Then he surprised her even further. "Shannon, do you know the Olsons?" he asked. "I understand they were friends of your grandmother's."

"Yes, I do. I was out here just the other day, visiting with Marge."

"Come on then. I think they might appreciate a friendly face when they hear about Booker's death." Grayson shut the door of the cruiser, and they headed back toward the main area.

"Good morning, Chief," Marge called as they approached the shed where the Olsons were sitting. "Would you like a cup of coffee or hot chocolate? And I've got fresh doughnuts. I know how you policemen like your doughnuts," she added slyly.

"I do love yours, Marge. Maybe later. Is there somewhere we can talk?" Grayson glanced around at the nearby customers. "Privately?"

Alarm flashed across Marge's features. She clutched Dick's arm. "Is something wrong?" Her voice dropped to a whisper. "Is it Finn? Has something happened to Finn?"

Shannon was sure that as a mother, she would react in exactly the same way if approached by a policeman wanting to talk in private.

"Yeah, Chief, don't keep us in suspense. What's up?" Despite Dick's gruff tone, his eyes were wide with fear.

Grayson lowered his voice. "It's not Finn. But I do assure you we need to talk in private."

Marge glanced helplessly at the cash register. She waved her hands around. "What am I going to do about this? I can't just go off and leave it. We've got a lot of people wanting to check out."

"Is there someone else who can take over?" Grayson asked.

"Chaz is out with the hayride right now," Dick said. Someone in a snowman costume waddled by and Dick whistled and waved his arm. The snowman changed direction and came over to the table. The snowman removed the costume's round head and Shannon saw to her surprise that it was Hillary Jenkins.

"Hillary!" she exclaimed. "I didn't know you worked here."

"Whenever Kate doesn't need me." She waved the head. "Nice outfit, huh?"

"I never would have recognized you."

Hillary turned to Dick. "What do you need, boss?"

"Can you run the cash register for a few minutes? Marge and I have something we need to take care of."

"I'd be glad to." She looked at the cash register. "Kate's is the same model. I'll do fine." Pulling off her red gloves, she cheerfully rang up a tree sale for a family who had been waiting.

In a quiet corner near the barn, away from the crowd, the Chief said, "I've got some bad news. There's been an accident here on the farm. Gary Booker is dead."

Marge gasped, both hands flying to her face. Shannon quickly put her arm around Marge.

"How the heck did you find out about it before we did?" Dick barked, his glare encompassing Shannon as well as the chief.

"Michael Stone and I found him," Shannon explained. "Michael called the chief, and by the time I got back to the parking lot, he was already here." That wasn't exactly true; she'd had time to send the twins away before the chief arrived. She'd have them call Grayson later to tell him anything or anyone they noticed while romping through the trees. She fervently hoped they had seen nothing related to the case.

"When did you last see Gary?" Grayson asked.

Dick shrugged. "About an hour and a half ago, I think. It was after the first hayride. He went out to the fields, and I just assumed he was helping customers with their trees. What happened to him anyway?"

Grayson flashed a look at Shannon to keep quiet. "The coroner needs to examine the body before I can release that information."

Dick hung his head and Shannon swore she saw his lips tremble behind that thick beard. Marge was sobbing openly now, drawing curious glances from passersby. *They must be devastated that their primary employee and surrogate son is dead,* Shannon thought.

Her eyes met Grayson's. "Why don't you two go on into the house?" the chief suggested. "I see the coroner arriving now. I'll be back in a while to give you an update."

The coroner's van and two more cruisers came rumbling up the dirt drive.

"But what about our customers?" Dick said.

"We're not letting anyone new in," Grayson explained. "We'll just let folks get their trees and leave, and my boys will question them on the way out."

"Why do they have to be questioned?" Dick asked. The chief shook his head, refusing to answer.

Jake Stager approached at a fast clip, his reporter's instincts alerted by the arrival of official vehicles. "What's going on, Chief?" he asked, flashing his press credentials.

Grayson swallowed a sigh of exasperation. "Press already?"

"I was here covering the event," Jake explained. "The Christmas kickoff." He pulled out his pad and pen, ready to take notes.

Grayson sighed again. "All I'm going to say is there has been an unattended death. I'll make a statement later, OK?"

Jake watched the coroner and several policemen head off into the tree farm. "Is the scene out there?"

"Don't even think about it." Grayson set his hat firmly on his head and strode after the coroner.

"Do you know anything about it, Shannon?" Jake asked.

She shook her head. "You better listen to Grayson. Disobeying him can be pretty unpleasant. Let's go inside, Marge. I'll make you and Dick tea."

Jake snorted. "I suppose I'll have my tenth cup of hot chocolate and wait." To Marge he added, "Not that it's not great hot chocolate. And I love those doughnuts."

She flapped a hand of dismissal at him, allowing Shannon to guide her toward the house. Dick followed in his motorized wheelchair.

In the kitchen, Shannon boiled water and made tea for the Olsons, who sat quietly, still immersed in stunned disbelief. Marge clutched her knitting, but she didn't make a single stitch. Dick gently stroked the purring tiger cat curled up on his lap. He reminded Shannon of other gruff men she'd known. Their harsh manner usually was just a protective shell masking a too-tender heart. Unfortunately, others often saw only the exterior. Dick was probably thinking about Gary—and his real son, Finn. No doubt he adored his son but hadn't the least idea how to bridge the ever-widening gap between them.

Shannon had just poured and prepared three cups of tea when her cellphone rang. Excusing herself, Shannon stepped into the hallway and dug the phone out of her jeans pocket. It was Essie.

She sounded frantic. "Shannon, we're slammed and I'm all by myself."

Shannon mentally reviewed the schedule. She had put Carrie on for today, right? "Where's Carrie?"

"She called in sick. I thought I could handle things OK until you got here this afternoon, but it's crazy. Can you come now?"

Shannon thought quickly. "I can't, but I'll call the twins and ask them to come in."

"Thank you so much," Essie exclaimed, relieved. She fell silent, and in the expectant pause that followed, Shannon could sense the questions she wanted to ask.

"I can't explain right now," Shannon said. "There's been an emergency at the farm, and I sent the twins home. So they're available."

"Oh, OK. Oops, got to go. Someone needs me." Shannon was thankful when Essie hung up without pressing for more information. She called the twins, who agreed to go straight to the store.

"I'll make it up to you both," Shannon told Alec, who had answered.

In a terrific display of maturity, Alec turned the focus back to her. "Don't worry about it, Mum. We're not little kids, but we are concerned about you. Are you doing OK?"

Shannon took a deep breath. "I'm fine, really. It's the Olsons I'm worried about."

"Yeah, the whole thing stinks. Call me later if you need a ride."

"Please don't say anything to Essie about Gary's death." Shannon ended the call as she walked back into the kitchen, blinking tears from her eyes. Her beautiful children never failed to amaze her.

The Olsons were drinking their tea, and Shannon was glad to see the liberal sugar she had added was bringing color to their faces. "Marge, Dick. I need to ask you something. Where's Finn? He really should be with you at a time like this." She braced herself for an answer ranging from angry to upset.

The Olsons exchanged glances, but neither seemed disturbed by her question, she was glad to see. "We haven't seen Finn for a couple of days," Marge finally admitted. She grimaced. "Ever since he and Gary got into it again."

"Where did he go?"

Marge shrugged. "To stay with friends, probably. He knows a lot of people around here."

Dick's tone was rueful. "I was hard on the boy. Maybe too hard." Perhaps the loss of Gary was making them reconsider their allegiance to their son, although both were surprisingly casual about knowing his whereabouts. Maybe after five years of his absence, they were used to his independence.

"It might not be a bad idea to give him a call," she suggested gently. Neither answered, so she dropped the subject.

Shannon felt ready to float away on a river of tea by the time Chief Grayson and Michael came back to the house. She gratefully led them to the kitchen, hoping she could leave soon. She needed to get to the store. Marge's sister and husband were due to arrive any minute, and they would take over caring for the Olsons' needs.

Grayson refused refreshments and a seat, choosing instead to remain standing. Behind him, Michael leaned in the doorway, arms crossed, watching.

"I'm going to make a statement to the press shortly, but I wanted to talk to you folks first." Grayson took a deep breath and both Olsons leaned forward, hanging on his every word. "It appears that Gary Booker was fatally shot— probably by accident—this morning while walking along the fence line. Shot with a bow and arrow, that is—not a gun."

Marge's jaw dropped and Dick swore softly under his breath. "By who?" Dick demanded, almost spitting the words out. A vein pulsed in his forehead. "We don't allow hunting on our property."

"We believe it was a stray arrow from the hunting area adjoining your land. It's turkey season, and we think the arrow is the type used in hunting fowl. We won't know for sure until the autopsy is complete."

"So what are you going to do about it?" Dick jabbed his forefinger at the chief with each word. "Idiot hunters! Don't even identify what they're shooting at! Stupid, stupid, stupid! Somebody's going to pay for this!" He picked up his cup and threw it against the wall, smashing it. Tea and shards of china rained down onto the floor. The tiger cat on Dick's lap bolted for a safer region of the house.

Marge shrieked and dropped her knitting, her shoulders quaking. Shannon patted her on the back, trying to comfort the older woman even though her own heart was pounding from the shock of Dick's action. Now she knew where Finn got his volatile temper.

"That's enough of that, Olson," Grayson snarled. "I know you're upset, and I don't blame you, but throwing things won't help, will it?"

Dick backed down, his palms raised in supplication. "I'm sorry, Chief. Being laid up with this bum leg makes me feel so helpless. I just want to—" He clenched his hands into fists again, demonstrating what he'd like to do to Gary's murderer. "I can't even help you find who did this."

"We're investigating; you have my word on that. We're going to locate each and every hunter who used that land today. You take care of your wife and leave the rest to us." Grayson hitched up his belt and adjusted his hat.

"Now I'd better go and slake the curiosity of the vultures waiting outside. The press," he added, realizing they might not understand what he was referring to.

Jake happened upon a more significant story than Christmas trees and hayrides today. Good for him. He's not so bad.

The chief paused in the doorway. "Shannon. Michael. Thanks for your quick work and assistance today. Come by the station later and give us your formal statements."

A compliment from the chief. Christmas miracle indeed!

9

Shannon was exhausted by the time she retired that evening. After the tumultuous events of the morning, they'd been swamped at the store right until closing. She was glad of that. Being busy had kept her thoughts and emotions about Gary Booker's death at bay.

Heaving a sigh of gratitude, she put on her thickest flannel nightgown and crawled into bed, pulling the down quilt up to her nose. There was nothing cozier than a warm bed on a cold night. The drapes in front of the French doors to the balcony were pulled back, revealing a view of moonlight shining on the snow. The snow cover magnified the moon's pale glow, making the night almost as bright as day.

She gazed out at the serene countryside, willing peace of mind to follow relaxation of body. Despite her best efforts to think only about pleasant topics, the memory of discovering Gary's body flashed into her mind. The stomach-turning shock of it. The waste and tragedy. Perhaps she hadn't liked him and had despised the trouble he seemed to leave in his wake, but no one deserved to die like that. Shot by an arrow right in the heart. Death had been quick, thankfully, according to what she had heard from Michael and Grayson. At least Gary hadn't suffered.

She sat bolt upright. *Shot in the heart, with an arrow. Like Cupid.* Was it some kind of a symbolic gesture?

No, that was crazy. She flopped back down onto her pillow. It was a hunting accident, plain and simple. A zealous hunter had shot at his target and the arrow had gone wild. She'd heard of stranger things. A woman wearing white mittens had been mistaken for a white-tailed deer and was fatally shot in her own backyard in Maine, for gosh sake.

With any luck, Chief Grayson would be able to track down the responsible party. Or maybe someone would come forward and admit they had been hunting on the adjacent property and had a shot go astray. In spite of safety training, some accidents occurred when hunters got excited and fired off bullets or arrows without clearly identifying the target.

Despite these logical conclusions, Shannon tossed fitfully, unable to get comfortable. Something wasn't right. Something she couldn't put her finger on.

She sat upright again, galvanized by a new thought. Michael. She'd talk to Michael, and he'd either reassure her that yes, Gary's death was an accident, or help her prove it had been cold-blooded, premeditated murder. She glanced at the clock. Too late to call tonight. She'd wait until morning.

Shannon gave a huge yawn and felt every part of her body relax, including her churning thoughts. Now she could sleep.

*　　*　　*

Sunday morning, before Shannon even thrust a toe out of her warm covers onto the cold floor, she picked up her cellphone. She had slept surprisingly well, but upon first light, her eyes had popped right open, her brain immediately going into gear. She had a mysterious death to investigate. Maybe. She eagerly called Michael.

"Good morning," Michael greeted her, his voice slightly gravelly with sleep. "You're up early."

Shannon looked out the French doors at the pink-tinged clouds heralding the dawning day and laughed. "Earlier than I had planned, for sure, on a Sunday morning. Can I tempt you with a homemade breakfast? I have something to run by you."

"Hmm." He pretended to consider. "Depends on what you're making. I'm pretty fussy."

Shannon laughed again. "You are not. I was thinking waffles and sausage with real maple syrup."

"How can I say no? Be there in half an hour."

Shannon put the phone down and smiled. Even a short conversation with Michael made her feel good. Aside from Coleen Douglas back in Scotland, he had become her best friend.

And a devilishly handsome one too! Shannon could just hear Coleen's voice. Coleen had been trying to match Shannon up with Michael since her arrival in Apple Grove. It was a little too soon to say, but Shannon had a feeling that Coleen might get her wish.

Och, away with you, lass! With a chuckle, Shannon pushed back the covers and stood up. She'd better hurry if she wanted to shower, dress, and start breakfast before Michael arrived.

Deborah was pouring herself a cup of coffee when Shannon walked into the kitchen. "I'm taking over," Shannon said. "Why don't you just relax with the newspaper in your sitting room?" She explained that Michael was coming to breakfast, and she would make a serving for Deborah too. The twins wouldn't be up for a while, but she'd leave batter for them as well as sausage.

"How nice of you, Shannon," Deborah said. Carrying her mug, she went to the front door to get the Sunday paper.

Sausage sizzled in a frying pan, and Shannon was whipping up waffle batter when Deborah came back into the kitchen, pale-faced and clutching the newspaper. She thrust it under Shannon's nose with a shaking hand. On the front page, the news was printed in huge letters: "Apple Grove Man Killed in Hunting Accident."

Jake had apparently filed his story.

"You and Michael found Gary Booker dead? How horrible!" Deborah exclaimed. She had been off the day before.

"Yes. Michael and I found him." Shannon grimaced. "Fortunately, the twins weren't with us when we found the body."

Deborah sank down into a chair. "Poor you." She shook her head. "What a terrible experience. I can't imagine." She stared into space, her expression bleak. "And the poor Olsons. They must be really upset to have one of their workers killed right there on their property."

"He was more than a worker. He practically ran the place." Shannon poured batter into the hot waffle iron and closed the lid. She'd been hungry when she got up, but now the thought of eating sickened her.

Michael tapped at the back door and came in. Under his winter coat, he wore a tweedy blue wool sweater that brought out the color of his eyes. "Smells wonderful in here," he said, smiling broadly. The smile dropped when he noticed the women's grim faces and the newspaper sitting on the table.

He picked it up and folded it, hiding the front page. "How about this? Let's have a nice breakfast before we talk or even think about Gary Booker." He shook a finger of mock reproof at Shannon and Deborah. "And that's an order."

While enjoying plates of crisp waffles smothered in butter and maple syrup with tasty sausage links on the side, conversation turned to Christmas plans.

"I found a recipe for Christmas pudding," Deborah announced. "And I also bookmarked a video on YouTube that shows me how to make it step-by-step. The BBC produced it, actually."

"YouTube? Really?" Shannon said with amusement. Deborah didn't use the computer in the study very often, claiming to find it confusing.

"Yes. Alec helped me find it. What a wonderful invention the Internet is."

"What exactly is in Christmas pudding?" Michael asked, spearing another waffle off the serving platter. He lavished it with butter and maple syrup and took a big, appreciative bite.

"Let's see," Deborah said, ticking the ingredients off on her fingers. "Dried fruit, apples and oranges, almonds, eggs, spices, brandy, suet—"

"Wait a sec," Michael said, sounding incredulous. "The brandy sounds good but did you say suet? The fatty white stuff I put on my bird feeder in winter?"

Deborah nodded. "Absolutely. That's what holds the pudding together and gives it a rich flavor."

"Take my word for it, you're going to love everything about this Christmas dinner," Shannon added. With a saucy wink, she popped the last morsel of sausage on her plate into her mouth.

Deborah's eyes widened. "Oh, will you be joining us, Michael?"

"Yes, ma'am. Looking forward to it."

Michael smiled at Shannon, and for a moment, she forgot all about the dreadful business of Gary Booker's death. Instead, she allowed the warmth in his gaze to fill her with joy. How she treasured the opportunity to spend time with her dearest ones during the most magical time of the year! And that category definitely included Michael, she realized, with a little jolt of her heart. *Does he feel the same?*

Deborah beamed with satisfaction as she got up from the table. "I'll just pick up these plates and leave you two alone."

After helping Deborah clean up, Shannon refilled their mugs and sat down.

"What's on your mind, Shannon?" Michael asked.

She took a sip of her coffee, unsure how to begin. "I'm beginning to think Gary's death was no accident," she finally blurted. "I have nothing concrete to go on, really, just a feeling. Maybe I subliminally noticed something at the site. Something that doesn't fit the chief's theory." Breath held, she waited for Michael's answer. She hoped he would tell her she was just imagining things and Gary's death was an unfortunate accident.

"You know what?" he said. "I think you're right. In fact, I've been thinking about it since last night."

"Me too!" Shannon exclaimed. "I had trouble getting to sleep."

Michael set his mug on the table and pulled out a pen. "Do you have a piece of paper?"

After Shannon found some paper in a drawer, Michael quickly sketched lines and circles on the page. "This represents the fence line," he said, running his finger over the makeshift diagram. "This is the tree where we found Gary, and then his tracks came this way. The arrow hit him here and he fell back against the tree. At least, that's what the footprints looked like." He drew another line coming from Gary's right, where the adjacent land lay. "To hit him in the chest, the arrow would have had to come from that direction. When I looked that way, I saw a number of big trees that would likely stop an arrow."

"And when I looked over the fence," Shannon added, "I didn't see any human or turkey tracks over there. The arrow would have had to come quite a distance then."

Michael studied the sketch. "I suppose the arrow could have hit him, spun him around, and he could have pulled himself into a sitting position before dying. But that seems far-fetched."

Shannon traced a trajectory line on the paper from inside the farm to Gary's body. "If we assume a straight shot, the arrow must have come from around there. Somewhere in the Christmas trees. But a location with a clear view of the fence line."

Michael whistled and shook his head. "That was a pretty bold move, if so. With all those people around ... strange that no one noticed someone carrying a bow. They're pretty good-sized."

"It could have been hidden somewhere. And that would

definitely mean premeditation," Shannon said. "I think we should go back to the farm after church and look around. I'll bring my camera." She smiled mischievously. "We have a perfect excuse. We never did cut our tree."

"I agree we should go and take another look, especially since the snow is melting. No harm done if we don't find anything."

Deborah bustled into the room. "Telephone, Shannon. It's Betty. It sounds urgent."

— 10 —

Shannon quickly picked up the phone. "Betty. Is everything all right?"

"The important question is, how are you? I just read the newspaper."

"Say no more. Yes, it was awful. I was so caught up I forgot to get my tree, so Michael and I have to go back out there today." No need to tell Betty her intention of investigating.

"I'm in pure shock. Not that I knew Gary that well, but he had dinner at the inn a couple of nights ago. And now he's dead. I just can't wrap my mind around it. Such an outgoing and good-looking man."

"That's right, Carrie mentioned going to dinner there when they left the shop the other night." She gulped. Poor Carrie. She had called in sick yesterday, but by now she had to know about Gary's death. How was she coping with it? Shannon felt like a heel for not thinking of her sooner. "Thanks for reminding me. I'd better check on Carrie. He was her boyfriend."

"She might not be as upset as you'd think," Betty said cryptically. She lowered her voice. "I have to go. Customers are coming down the stairs to check out. Listen, if you do go to the farm, can you bring me another tree? A nice, fat four-footer for the lobby. I'll pay you, of course. And maybe you can have a late lunch here? I've got some new recipes I'm trying out."

"Yes to both. See you later." Shannon couldn't wait to hear what had happened at dinner between Carrie and Gary. She made a mental note to check on Carrie later. Even if Gary was a heel, it hurt to lose someone you loved. She knew that very well indeed.

*   *   *

When Shannon pulled Old Blue into the parking lot at the farm, the first thing she noticed was something missing: customers. There was nary a car in the main lot and just a few vehicles behind the barn. Those no doubt belonged to the Olsons and their workers. Shannon recognized Dick's van, parked next to the green pickup Gary had used.

"Where is everyone?" Shannon asked Michael.

He sighed. "I was afraid this would happen. The so-called accident has driven away all the customers. I'm sure Mommy and Daddy are worried about an arrow hitting little Johnny or Julie while they're picking out a Christmas tree. And you really can't blame them."

"Oh my. They'll stay away until hunting season ends. And when is that?"

"For turkey hunting, December thirty-first."

"In other words, well after Christmas tree buying season." Shannon opened the driver's side door, which creaked loudly as always, perhaps even a little worse in the cold weather. "This is just going to kill the Olsons' business. But I think I have an idea that will help."

Marge answered the front door at their knock, looking even more downcast and glum than ever. "Oh, hello, Shannon.

Mr. Stone. Come on in." Opening the door wide, she turned
and shuffled back to the warm, sunlit kitchen. Dick grunted
a greeting from his wheelchair near the picture window, the
tiger cat back in his lap. One end of the big table was strewn
with what appeared to be ledgers, bank statements, and other
paperwork. A big, old-fashioned electronic calculator stood
ready, complete with a roll of white paper. Marge must have
been doing her bookkeeping.

"Have a seat," Marge said, gesturing toward seats at the
other end of the table. "Would you like tea or coffee?" She
pushed a plate of doughnuts toward them. "Help yourself.
I've got plenty."

"I would, but I've just eaten a huge breakfast," Shannon
said. "A cup of tea would be nice."

Michael requested coffee before taking a seat in one of
the chairs.

Dick nodded toward the rows of Christmas trees
stretching into the distance. "Not a single customer today.
Only good news is that trees don't spoil. We can sell 'em
next year—well, except the ones already cut." His irritable
expression deepened into a scowl.

"That's rough," Michael sympathized.

"I have an idea," Shannon said. "How about bringing
trees into town and selling them there? I have room at the
side of my shop."

Marge paused in lifting the teacup to her mouth. "You'd
let us do that? Really?"

"That's a nice offer," Dick said, his face softening into a
near-smile. "What would we owe you?"

"Not a thing. The space is empty since the gardens are

dormant. And besides, your trees will attract more customers to my shop." Perhaps framing her offer as a benefit to herself would help the proud Olsons accept it. "You should start today. The tree lighting on the green is tonight, and there will be hundreds of people downtown."

The annual lighting of the gigantic fir drew people from towns surrounding Apple Grove as well as residents and visitors. The gold "memory stars" that people attached to the tree before the ceremony in memory of departed loved ones were an especially nice feature. Shannon had purchased one in memory of her husband, John. All proceeds went to help the needy at Christmas.

Excited, Dick rolled his wheelchair toward the back door. The cat jumped down and ran off; Shannon wondered when the poor thing would give up sitting in his lap. "I'll have Chaz and Tim start cutting and loading right away," Dick said.

"The reason I'm here," Shannon said, "is to get my tree. In all the ... excitement ... yesterday, I forgot all about it."

Dick paused the chair. "If you need a saw, check in the barn. They're all in there."

Shannon noticed Marge glancing toward the pile of paperwork. She knew what it was like to be interrupted in the middle of doing bookkeeping. "Go ahead and do what you need to do, Marge," she said. "We'll be out of your hair in a minute."

"If you don't mind." Marge settled herself at the other end of the table. "I'm having trouble reconciling the deposits to the daily sales record. Somehow they're not matching up." She gave a dry chuckle. "I guess doing books wasn't Gary's strong point."

Shannon had the unpleasant suspicion that Gary had indeed known what he was doing. A common problem was when employees "borrowed" funds, namely cash, and put them back later. That was one reason why the deposits wouldn't match the sales. But there was no point in upsetting Marge by saying so.

After finishing their drinks, Shannon and Michael went out to the barn. Across the parking lot, Chaz and Tim were already stacking cut trees onto a trailer attached to the pickup truck. Inside the dim barn with its pleasant mingled aromas of horse and hay, Shannon and Michael hesitated, disconcerted. Other than an open area near the horse stall, the space was packed with boxes, barrels, tools, and equipment.

"Where do you suppose the saws are?" Michael mused.

"I should have brought one. We have a couple in the garden shed."

Roscoe, the draft horse, hung his big head over the stall door and snorted a greeting.

"Hi, Roscoe," Shannon said, stroking his big velvety nose. He swung his head, butting her hand affectionately.

"I have an idea," Michael said. "I'll start on the left and you start on the right. We'll work our way around."

Shannon gave Roscoe a farewell caress and began systematically examining the barn contents on her assigned side. Bags of horse feed. A barrel of nails. Stacked crates of glass milk bottles. They must have had cows in the past. A bucket of turkey feathers.

Turkey feathers. She recognized their distinctive pattern of white stripes on a dark brown background. "Hey, Michael. Come over here."

He trotted over. "Did you find them?"

"No. But look at these." She pointed at the feathers.

"Someone who lives here hunts, obviously," he said. "And that means there could be a bow and arrow on the property too. Unless they used a gun, of course." He picked up the bucket by its handle. "Let's put them somewhere where they won't get thrown out. Just until we know we don't need them." He tucked the bucket behind an old wooden double yoke covered with dust and cobwebs and draped a burlap sack over it.

"Can I help you?" a male voice said.

Shannon jumped. Even the unflappable Michael flinched a little. They slowly turned around. Finn stood in the doorway, wearing a down vest over a plaid flannel shirt and jeans. His hair was standing on end like he'd just rolled out of bed. Even in the dim light of the barn, Shannon could see big circles under his eyes and a chin that hadn't seen a razor for a couple of days.

She pasted a big, innocent smile on her face. "Um, we're looking for the handsaws. Your dad sent us out here to look."

Michael gestured at the sheer volume of stuff surrounding them. "You can see it's no easy task."

With a tut-tut of his tongue and shake of his head, Finn crossed the barn and went right to a box near the back entrance. Reaching inside, he pulled out a yellow-handled bucksaw. "Is this what you're looking for?"

"Yes. Thank you." Shannon took the saw. Closer to Finn, she saw further evidence of poor sleep and a troubled mind etched into his young, handsome face. "How are you doing, Finn?"

He shrugged. "Not great." He took a deep breath. "I

know you mean well, but I really don't want to talk about it." Turning away, he began to coil a rope that was lying loose near the horse stall.

As Shannon and Michael made their escape, she cheerfully called out despite the snub, "See you later, Finn." He merely grunted an answer. Perhaps he was more like his father than Betty and others believed.

"You know, we're going to need some help getting your giant tree back to the parking lot, since we don't have Alec and Lara today," Michael commented. "Let's ask the guys to help."

"Good idea," Shannon said. Perhaps she could subtly question them at the same time. First she grabbed a small backpack containing coffee and Deborah's raspberry-filled cookies from inside Old Blue. She and Michael could have a little picnic in the snow while investigating.

"Hey, Mrs. McClain," Chaz called as they approached the truck and trailer. He and Tim were tying down the load. "Thanks for letting us sell next to your store."

"Yeah," Tim put in. "There'll be a lot more people downtown." Like Chaz, Tim was a wiry, good-looking youth.

"And they've got the best coffee right there," Chaz said to Tim.

"Cool."

"Glad to do it," Shannon said. She pointed to her tree, the tallest noble fir in the row. "Can you two come out and help us get that cut and loaded on my truck? I don't think we can handle it ourselves."

Chaz whistled when he spotted the tree she was indicating. "She's a beaut. Great choice, Mrs. McClain. We'll be glad to help."

The four of them walked through the rows, heading for Shannon's tree. "Not many customers today, I see," Shannon said, breaking the ice regarding the mysterious death.

"Like none!" Chaz exclaimed. He shook his head. "Everyone got scared off."

"Yeah, man," Tim said, his eyes wide. "The whole thing was freaky. Shot right in the heart with an arrow." He demonstrated. "Pow!"

"Did you two see anything?" Michael asked.

They both shrugged in that elaborate yet nonchalant way young people perfect with much practice.

"I was loading trees all day," Tim said. "I didn't leave the parking lot."

"I didn't go into the field until I took that hayride for Gary. And by then, he was already dead, I guess." Chaz's face was pale and serious. "It could have been us. Or one of the little kids." He shuddered.

Unless Gary was the sole target.

"That would have been really rough," Tim agreed.

"Don't take this the wrong way," Michael said. "But do either of you bow-hunt turkey?"

"I don't hunt, man," Tim said. "My father and brother hunt deer, but with guns."

"Like, as in the arrow that killed Gary?" Chaz asked. He wasn't stupid. "What—you think someone used a bow and arrow lying around the farm?"

Eager to curb rumors, Shannon said, "We saw some loose turkey feathers in the barn, that's all."

"Gotta be Finn," Chaz said. "He hunts." He lowered his voice, although there was no one around for miles. "Are you two investigating again?" He shot a look of glee at Tim. "I knew it wasn't an accident. Gary was a jerk to everyone who worked here." He hastily crossed himself. "Not to speak ill of the dead."

Tim had no such reservations. "Yeah. He thought he owned the place. No wonder Finn hated him. And what a dog! He hit on my girlfriend when she came by to visit one day."

Uh-oh. We'd better contain this. By Michael's raised brows, Shannon knew he shared her concern.

"Look, guys, no one's saying that Gary was shot deliberately," Shannon assured them. "I saw the feathers and was just curious."

Michael chimed in. "Please let the police investigate. You wouldn't want to cause trouble for someone who's innocent, would you?"

"No, I wouldn't," Chaz said solemnly, perhaps remembering his own brush with the law.

"Yeah, we'll keep a lid on it," Tim assured them.

With the help of the two young men, they quickly got the big tree cut down.

"I need to find a smaller one for a friend," Shannon said, giving herself and Michael an excuse to linger.

"We'll take this back and load it for you," Chaz said.

"It's as long as the truck," Tim said with a laugh. "But no worries, we'll use lots of rope."

After the voices of the young men faded, Shannon and Michael headed for the tree where Gary's body had been found. Yellow crime-scene tape bordered the adjacent area, but Shannon and Michael were more concerned about the property on the other side of the fence.

The snow was rapidly disappearing, but impressions,

including footprints, remained. They could easily see Gary's prints approaching along the fence line and stopping at the tree. Shannon pulled out her digital camera and made some adjustments. "With the right settings, I'll be able to visually deepen any marks in the snow," she said, "even though it looks like they would photograph plain white." Clicking away, she made a photographic record of the footprints.

Careful not to obliterate any traces of the dead man, Shannon and Michael next peered over the fence into the adjacent land. As Shannon had noted yesterday, it didn't appear anyone or any creature had ventured near the fence.

Again, Shannon captured the scene on the camera. "I'll enhance these and see if there's anything we're missing with the naked eye. But I really don't think so."

"I'm impressed," Michael said. "I could use you on some of my cases."

"Ooh, that sounds intriguing," Shannon said lightly, secretly flattered. "Now that we're here again, what do you think of an arrow coming from those woods?"

"My memory was correct. Those big trees would deflect an arrow. See?" He pointed out the trees' random zigzag pattern that would be impossible to shoot around. Shannon snapped a couple of shots.

"In the interest of being thorough, let's walk along the fence line a bit," Michael suggested.

They strolled slowly along, searching on both sides for clues, footprints, anything out of place. The line of noble firs followed on their left, broken only by sawed trunks like missing teeth and one wide aisle used by workers to bring a tractor or mower through. "There's where we need to look," Shannon said. "That spot is clear all the way to the maple."

"You're right," Michael said. "But look at this. Someone's been trespassing on the tree farm."

Up ahead, the wire fence, made of grid-like squares, had been neatly cut away near a pole and pulled back onto the adjacent land. The resulting gap was wide enough to allow someone to slip through. Shannon looked down. There were no other prints up to this point besides hers and Michael's, so the police hadn't seen this. In contrast, the ground near the opening looked trampled.

"Let's not go any closer," Michael said. "The shooter may have come in this way."

"I wonder how long the fence has been like that," she said.

"After it snowed the last time," Michael pointed out. "Look how the bottom edge of the fence moved the snow aside." Indeed, it looked from here that the edge had been dragged across existing snow, scraping it into a pile much like a plow would.

Shannon put on her longest zoom setting and shot pictures of the vandalized fence. Moving as close as they dared without destroying any possible evidence, they tried to discern where the footsteps led. A couple of sets leading into the row of trees and coming back to the fence were clearly defined. But near the Christmas trees, too many other people had trampled the area. Shannon did get several shots of the individual prints heading to and from the fence.

"The problem with this time of year," she noted, "is that everyone wears thick boots and most have the same kind of sole. Waffle tread." She held her foot up in demonstration.

"True," Michael agreed. "Mine too. The footprints will likely only be supplemental evidence. Unless someone has a giant foot, like Sasquatch."

Michael's reference to the legendary Pacific Northwest beast reputed to be hair-covered, ten feet tall, and with feet twenty-four inches long made Shannon laugh. "Do you believe in Bigfoot? Those stories remind me of the Loch Ness Monster. Just enough sightings to make you wonder."

Michael's eyes twinkled. "I don't, but I've met some old-timers who swear a friend of theirs had an encounter."

"Isn't that always the way? It's a friend or friend of a friend who actually had the experience."

They retraced their steps to the maple where Gary had been found, then sighted an angle into the tree farm and began to walk in that direction. To one side of the wide aisle, the trees had been cut extensively, leaving open ground with short stumps hidden by snow. Shannon found that sliding her boots through the snow helped her identify any obstacles before tripping over them. "With the trees gone right here," she pointed out, "there wouldn't be many customers hanging around."

Michael stopped and gazed back toward the maple, making sure it was still in view. "That's true. It's looking more and more like someone stalked Gary."

"It's just going to be hard to prove it," Shannon said. "Hundreds of people have come through here."

"Don't give up yet. One thing about a murder, no matter how well planned, is that the killer usually makes a mistake somewhere along the line. Especially if the murder is precipitated by emotion of some kind."

Shannon thought about all the cases she'd solved. Each killer had wanted something, and in his or her disordered mind, it had made perfect sense to eliminate someone else in pursuit of their desire. "Love, greed, revenge, or insanity," Shannon mused. "The four most common reasons for murder."

"Yeah, unless it's gang warfare or a mob hit," Michael said. "And I don't see any signs of that kind of criminal activity in this case. Yet." He pointed to a large, fat Christmas tree on the edge of the cleared area. "Let's look there. It's a little bit elevated and sheltered from view." He looked back at the maple. "About forty yards. Not a bad bow shot."

The snow near the tree had been stamped by footprints of all sizes, including many with the ubiquitous waffle-tread soles. Regardless, Shannon and Michael carefully examined the area around the tree for clues. As Shannon was peering under the thick, low-lying bottom branches, almost ready to give up, the sun broke through the cloud cover and made the snow crystals sparkle and dance. The welcome light also illuminated something else: a flash of silver metal half-submerged in the snow.

11

"Michael, I've found something." Shannon pointed to the piece of metal resting in the snow. "I wonder what it is."

Michael broke off a small, feathery branch and carefully brushed snow from around the object. The pointed piece of metal had two wings protruding from its cylindrical core. "It's an arrowhead. Take a picture, please. I'll call the chief."

"You must have him on speed dial," Shannon noted drily.

Grayson took a little persuading, and Shannon was glad Michael was handling the call. If it had been her, he probably would have refused to come despite the respect he seemed to finally have for her natural instincts. As it was, she could clearly hear him protesting since he seemed to be yelling. "Stone, we're busy working our way through the list of hunters who were on the open land Saturday. Who knew there were so many darn fools trying to shoot their own turkey rather than just go to the supermarket and buy one."

"Chief," Michael said, remaining patient with a heroic effort, "I doubt the killer signed the logbook. We found broken fence just a little ways up from where the body was. Did your guys see that?"

The chief was silent for a moment. "That's why Booker had wire cutters and a roll of wire with him."

Gary had been on his way to fix the fence. Oddly, Dick hadn't known that. In fact, no one knew where he had gone.

Shannon put the camera in her pack and pulled out the thermos of coffee, glad she had thought to bring it along. Despite the slight warm-up in temperature, she was getting chilled standing in one spot.

Michael made his most significant point. "Chief, there's no way the arrow came from the adjacent land. I've checked the trajectory. And we found the arrowhead in a spot that's a perfect sight line from the maple tree."

"*We?* I assume Shannon is with you?"

Michael winked and took the cup of hot coffee with a smile. "She sure is. She helped me figure out that something wasn't quite right with the arrow coming from the other side of the fence."

Grumbling—fortunately incoherent—came over the phone, and then the chief clearly said, "I'll be right out. Wait for me. And don't move that arrowhead!"

"Of course not. See you soon." Michael hung up and pocketed his phone. "The chief's a good guy, but he hates it when a simple case gets complicated." He sipped his coffee. "This hits the spot."

"Have a cookie." Shannon handed him one of the fat, sugar-sprinkled treats.

They had worked their way through the coffee and most of the cookies by the time Grayson and Officer Brownley showed up at the maple tree. Both wore heavy jackets, boots, and leather gloves. Shannon and Michael watched them leave the crime scene, obviously walking along the fence line to the broken spot. They returned and scanned the trees for Shannon and Michael, who waved. From their spot near the tree, they could see the two policemen perfectly. And in turn,

Shannon saw the chief's nod of grudging acceptance that indeed the arrow could have come from there.

"I see what you're saying, Stone," Grayson said as he and Brownley trudged up the slight slope to where they stood. He looked back toward the maple. "It would have been a clear shot from here. Where's the arrowhead?"

Shannon pointed it out, and the two policemen examined it closely, leaving it where it lay.

"Looks like a turkey arrowhead all right," Brownley noted. "They call those broadheads. We'll have to match it with the one from the body." He pulled out his own digital camera and took several shots. The chief handed him an evidence bag and, using gloved fingers, Brownley carefully plucked it from the snow and popped it inside. The chief sealed and initialed it.

"How'd you find this?" Grayson asked, waving the bag.

"I was searching under the tree and the sun reflected off it," Shannon answered. "It was only half buried."

The chief gave a heavy sigh. "I'd hate to think Gary Booker was murdered."

"We all would," Michael said.

"I'll have the state forensic team come up and do measurements," Grayson said. "They can figure distance and trajectory and drop, all that. We'll need to prove that someone could have hit him from here hard enough to kill him."

"Those arrows can be lethal," Brownley put in. "With today's bows, they're almost like bullets."

"Whoever it was, they were skilled," Michael said. "And quick. The farm was crawling with people that day."

"Maybe they came in through the fence," Shannon suggested, "and left that way."

"Good point. Brownley, you and Doan need to check that out. Follow the trail from the fence cut and see where it goes. Be careful not to wreck the tracks, OK?".

Brownley nodded. "I'll get him out here right away."

"You two didn't see anything suspicious from that direction, did you?" Grayson asked.

Shannon and Michael shook their heads. "I didn't see anyone on the way to our tree at all," Shannon said, "or walking down the fence line."

Michael concurred.

"What about the twins? They see anything?" Grayson's lip quirked in a one-sided smile. "I saw them leaving when we arrived."

Shannon's face flushed. Of course he had seen them. She should have had them talk to the chief last night. "I'll have them call you, Chief. I've been meaning to do that, but there hasn't been time."

Grayson relented. "I'm sure your first thought was to get them out of here. I know I'd feel the same way about my kids." He clapped Shannon on the shoulder. "Just have them call me tomorrow morning. Now that we think someone shot Booker from here, their statements are even more important."

"I'll do that," Shannon promised.

The foursome tramped toward the farmhouse, scanning the ground for further clues. The foot and horse traffic from the day before made it impossible to separate out any tracks amid the maze of Christmas trees. A candy wrapper, several cigarette butts, loose orange tape from tagged trees, and a baby's pacifier were the only items they found. Brownley bagged the wrapper and butts and picked up the tape to be discarded. Shannon took the pacifier, promising to give it to Marge for the lost-and-found. She could imagine the parents' dismay when the baby had first cried for his or her "dummy," as they called them in Scotland.

"Maybe it was Cupid's arrow," Brownley said in a surprising show of black, rather inappropriate humor. He flinched when Grayson glared at him, then muttered, "Sorry, Chief."

Shannon bit back a giggle, turning her face so Grayson wouldn't notice. A glance at Michael revealed he was also reluctantly amused.

As they entered the farmyard, Finn emerged from the barn, headed toward the parked vehicles. He had changed from his jeans and flannel; now he wore an orange wool hat and vest over camo jacket and pants. A canvas weapon bag hung from one shoulder. When he spotted the group, he stopped and waited.

"What's going on?" he asked. "I thought you were all done here."

Shannon studied him carefully, analyzing his expression and tone of voice. He seemed genuinely curious, if a bit annoyed, like any property owner might be. She and Michael hung back a little, out of Grayson's direct view. She wanted to hear this interview.

Instead of answering Finn's question, Grayson shot back, "Going hunting?"

"Yep, I sure am." Finn's raised brows conveyed succinctly that it wasn't anyone's business.

"What kind of hunting?" Grayson pressed.

"What are you asking? What I'm hunting for or what

method I'm using?" Finn's eyes glittered as he began to understand where this was heading.

"Both."

"Well, today I'm going turkey hunting. And yes, I use a bow and arrow. Doesn't destroy the bird like a shotgun does."

Either Finn was innocent or he was applying the reverse psychology that a murderer would surely distance himself from all suspicion. With that logic, openly admitting to using a bow and arrow would imply innocence.

"Interesting that you hunt when your folks have flocks of geese and ducks," Grayson noted. "Aren't those enough poultry for you?"

Finn sighed. "It's not about the meat per se, it's the sport." He smacked his lips in a crude imitation of an ignorant backcountry hick. "Right tasty though." He stood poised to escape, casting longing glances toward the van parked next to the barn. The farm truck and trailer were gone; Chaz and Tim must have left for town with their load of trees.

"Let me see your license," Grayson ordered. "You do have one, right?"

With another sigh, Finn shrugged off the case, setting it on the ground, and pulled out his wallet. He flipped it open. "Here you go. My turkey tag too."

Grayson handed them to Brownley, who studied them intently.

"You just came back to the country, right? How'd you get a turkey tag? Those are limited."

"Uh, the Internet? It works overseas too, believe it or not." His smile was snide.

Grayson bristled, his face turning dusky red. "No call to get smart with me, Finn. I could be questioning you down at the station."

"Look, Chief, all I know is Gary Booker got himself shot on my parents' property yesterday. I had nothing to do with it. I wasn't even anywhere near here all day. You can ask Mom and Dad if you want. Besides, wasn't it an accident? That's what the paper said." Finn smirked again. He didn't have to add that the paper had quoted the chief on the matter.

Grayson's face got even brighter red. He was no doubt embarrassed that he had come out so strongly in proclaiming the death an accident. "I will be talking to your parents, believe me. Where were you yesterday?"

"Hunting." At Grayson's frown, he added, "Not next door. Forty miles from here. Bob Misner's got land he lets me use."

"You get anything?"

"Nope. That's why I'm going out today."

Shannon remembered the feathers in the barn. "How many turkeys can you take?" she asked.

Both Grayson and Finn glared at her interruption. Brownley answered, "Two during open season. And that's what we're in right now."

"I got one the other day—on the land next to us, actually—so I have one left," Finn said.

"Did anyone see you on Misner's land?"

Finn shook his head. "I was the only one hunting that I know of. And before you ask, Bob wasn't home, so I didn't see him, either. And the site's way down a dead-end dirt road, so nobody goes out there."

Finn couldn't have picked a more isolated spot if he tried, Shannon reflected. Impossible to verify his time of arrival and departure, or even his presence at all.

"So you didn't see anyone at all yesterday?" Grayson's eyes narrowed in suspicion. "Gas station, maybe? Restaurant?"

The young man bit his lip, staring at the ground. Was he trying to think up a lie, drum up an alibi? "I did see one person. In the morning. I came back here late last night after I got done hunting and heard about Gary on the radio. I'd rather not drag her into this, though. She has nothing to do with it."

"You need to tell me who it is, Finn," the chief commanded in a deathly quiet voice. "Let us decide who is and isn't involved." His voice rose slightly as Finn hesitated. "You don't seem to realize how serious this is. We're possibly talking aggravated murder here." It was the most serious charge in Oregon.

Finn's face blanched. "Murder? I thought you were accusing me of shooting Booker by accident." He set his shoulders square and said, "All right. I'll tell you. I was with Carrie Weston."

— 12 —

Shannon had to bite her lip to keep from crying out. Her mind raced with questions. What was Finn's relationship with Carrie? Were they seeing each other again? But what about her involvement with Gary? She brought her attention back to what the chief was saying.

"I'll need to take a look at your bow and arrows," he said.

Finn picked up his canvas case, clutching it in his arms. "No way. Get a warrant."

The front door of the farmhouse burst open, and Marge and Dick appeared on the front porch. Taking in the situation—the police questioning their son—Marge ran toward them while Dick trundled behind in his chair. His voice reached them before he did when he roared, "What the heck is going on?"

"Mom. Dad. Go back in the house. I can take care of myself."

Dick, panting with anxiety and exertion as he rolled up, said, "This is our business too, son." His piercing eyes landed on Grayson. "Tell me what you're doing here, please."

Grayson shifted in discomfort under the other man's intense stare, scuffing one of his boots into the dirt. "We've got new information about Gary Booker's death."

"And they're accusing me of murdering him." Finn's tone was bitter. "Not that I wouldn't have liked to."

Marge shrieked, "Don't say that, Finn!" She turned on

the chief like a mother bear defending her lone cub. "First you tell us it's an accident, and now you're here arresting our son! How dare you?"

Grayson held both hands up, attempting to placate their wrath. "I'm not arresting anyone. Yet. We've found some new evidence, so we're asking further questions. That's all."

"Who found new evidence?" Dick barked. His eyes fell on Shannon and Michael. "Ah. Was it you two?"

Marge's mouth fell open. "Shannon?" Her large brown eyes held a look of betrayal.

Shannon's face flushed with guilt. "I'm sorry, Marge, but—"

Michael stepped in smoothly. "We aren't trying to implicate anyone, and, in fact, we have no opinion about who shot Gary. But it's plain that the arrow was shot by someone on the farm and not by hunters on the adjacent land as originally believed."

"Your theory may be verified once the forensics are completed," Grayson said, reinforcing his department's role in determining the facts.

"That's right," Michael continued, undisturbed in the least by Grayson's positioning. "We're seeking the truth, whatever that might be. So if Finn is innocent, there's no problem. Surely you want to know who killed Gary."

"Of course we do." Marge blinked back furious tears. "But I'm not sure how much more we can take. Everything's falling apart."

Finn dropped his bag again and put his arm around his mother. "I'm sorry, Mom. We'll get through this." His look at Grayson and Brownley held pure hatred. "Go ahead and get a warrant. In the meantime, I'm going to go call an attorney."

Grayson sighed and threw up his hands. "Go ahead, Finn, if that's what you need to do. In any case, we're going to continue to do our jobs. That's what we're paid for." He and Brownley stomped off toward their cruiser.

"Um, I need to pay you for my tree," Shannon said to Marge, pointing to the enormous fir tied to Old Blue. "And I want to get another tree for Betty, if that's OK." Shannon wasn't certain they would want anything to do with her, at least for a while. She still felt queasy with remorse over the turn events had taken. The last thing she wanted was to hurt her grandmother's friend by contributing to her son being thrown in jail.

"Oh, honey, we're not blaming you," Marge said. "And your offer to let us sell trees in town was a nice one. Why don't we call it even? You pick out a tree for Betty and we'll throw that in too."

"Are you sure?" Marge nodded and even Dick grunted in agreement. "Thanks. I'll do that. I love your trees."

With muted farewells, the Olsons turned as a unit and went back toward the house. Shannon and Michael watched for a moment until Michael said gently, "Why don't we get that tree and go? Let them regroup for a while."

"I feel so bad!" Shannon burst out. "I didn't think our investigation would end up going in this direction!"

Michael put his arm around her shoulders and led her toward the trees. "We did what we had to do. We couldn't ignore the evidence. Murder is a messy business, and unfortunately, there's a lot of spillover. Innocent bystanders—and innocent investigators too."

Shannon tried to enjoy the warm comfort of Michael's arm,

but her mind kept churning. *Finn has to be innocent—right?* He certainly had grounds to hate Gary for taking over the farm and influencing his parents. Motive ... check. Means ... check. Opportunity? That was the question. To all appearances, he hadn't been at the farm all day. But there was that broken fence.

With a supreme effort, she forced her thoughts away from Finn and the murder to a happier topic: Betty's tree. "How about that one?" she inquired, pointing to a fat, four-foot Douglas fir nearby. "It's just right for the inn lobby." She could picture it sitting in the wide bay window.

Michael still had the yellow saw in his left hand, and now he brandished it, saying, "Paul ... er ... Michael Bunyan at your service, madam."

Shannon broke away from Michael and grabbed the top of the tree, steadying it. "Let me see your best cutting technique, Mr. Bunyan!"

*   *   *

"That tree is perfect!" Betty exclaimed as Shannon entered the lobby, carrying the Douglas fir. She bustled around from behind the desk and helped Shannon place it beside the bay window. "When Tom gets home, he'll put it up for me."

Boxes of Victorian-themed decorations, garland, and lights sat nearby. The entire inn, with its ceiling frescos, silk- and velvet-upholstered furniture, and floral wallpapers, was decorated to complement the Queen Anne style of the building.

"Good. I thought it would be the right size and shape."

"Come on into the tearoom and check out our new menu."

Betty led the way to Shannon's favorite pink-upholstered

booth, the one with the snail salt and pepper shakers. The table arrangement today was a mix of feathery evergreens, baby's breath, and pink berries. As the teapot-shaped menu revealed, the tearoom had a focus on local foods. So did the dinner menu, which was served several nights a week in the cozy Fireplace Room, a new addition to the inn's amenities.

"This all looks yummy," Shannon said, scanning the menu. Walking around the farm in the fresh air had whetted her appetite. "I want one of each."

"We just got a professional panini machine," Betty said. "And since they're hot, paninis are great on cold winter days."

Livy, the waitress, brought them a steaming pot of tea and teacups and waited for their order.

"Hi, Livy. I'll have the butternut squash soup and the cheddar-and-apple panini," Shannon said. "Thank you." The squash, apples, and cheese all came from a nearby farm.

"Good choice," Betty said. "Please bring me the soup and the roast beef with blue cheese and onions. Thanks, dear." She smiled at Livy, who bustled away.

"That was my second choice," Shannon said.

"Let's swap halves then," Betty suggested. She poured them each a cup of steaming tea, and for a couple of minutes, Shannon just relaxed, absorbing the inn's quaint, old-fashioned atmosphere. In the background, classical Christmas music played softly. The air smelled of cinnamon and butter and sugar.

"So did you get your tree?" Betty asked.

"We sure did. I left it at the house, and Michael is going to help Alec set it up later. We found an ancient cast-iron tree stand in the attic that will work great for such a huge tree."

"Where is Michael? I'd hoped he would join us for lunch."

"He had a telephone appointment late this afternoon. Someone in Tokyo—it's already Monday there. Apparently his work doesn't slow down ever, even at Christmastime."

Betty indicated the tearoom, crammed full of patrons. "When you're in business for yourself, you have to make hay while the sun shines."

"That I understand. In fact, after this, I'm heading for the store. We're staying open a little later tonight because of the tree-lighting ceremony."

Livy soon brought their lunch, and Betty said a short blessing. In unspoken agreement, discussion of Gary Booker was left until after every delicious, savory morsel had been devoured.

"Tell Gertrude this was outstanding," Shannon said. Deborah's sister, Gertrude, was a chef at the inn.

"I sure will." Betty filled their teacups again. "How are you doing, Shannon?" She pushed Shannon's cup toward her and moved a stand holding Christmas-shaped short-breads a little closer to hand.

Shannon knew this was Betty's tactful way of checking in on her emotions and turmoil regarding the discovery of Gary Booker's body. "I'm OK. But I am concerned about Carrie. She seemed to really like Gary." While eating, Shannon had decided not to tell anyone, even close friends, about the new developments in the investigation, especially Finn being under suspicion. Although Betty wasn't a gossip, Shannon knew that rumors had a life of their own. Sometimes people assumed that if you were a suspect, you had to be guilty. She didn't want to ruin Finn's life if he was indeed innocent.

A sad expression crossed Betty's face. "Oh, I am so sorry for Carrie. What she must be going through."

"What happened when they had dinner here? I'm just trying to get a reading on the situation before I talk to her."

"They seemed happy enough at first. Carrie was just bubbling over with excitement when she introduced me to him." Betty shook her head. "Gary sure was charming. He even flirted with an old lady like me."

"Come on. You're very attractive."

Betty waved off the compliment. "Something went wrong during dessert. They were sitting in the corner, all lovey-like, if you know what I mean, when suddenly Carrie got up and stormed out. She did it so violently that the dishes rattled on the table and a glass of wine fell over. Gary got up immediately, paid the bill, and left."

"Think, Betty. Did anything happen before the argument?"

Betty frowned. "The only thing I can think of is Gary went to the restroom." Light dawned in her eyes. "Oh, I know. He stopped and talked to the waitress. Livy's sister, Amy. She's a young and lovely girl."

Gary Booker couldn't resist flirting with any woman who crossed his path, even while on a date. Shannon had the unsettling thought that this weakness may have gotten him killed.

*   *   *

After parking Old Blue behind the store, Shannon went around front to see how Chaz and Tim were making out with the tree sales.

"We're doing great, Mrs. McClain," Chaz said. "Tim's going back out to get another load."

"That's super," Shannon said. Despite it being Sunday afternoon, the sidewalks were bustling with people. Over on the green, the tree committee was getting ready for the lighting ceremony at six.

As she walked toward the front door, she saw Hillary coming down the street. The girl was walking three small poodles—or rather, they were walking her. "Whoa!" she cried, pulling them to a stop beside Shannon. For once, the young woman was smiling.

"Did you hear about my new job?" she asked. "I'm going to be working at Olson's Tree Farm full time. They even gave me a room." She laughed. "Pets are OK, but I prefer working with trees."

"How nice for you," Shannon said. "You seemed right at home the other day."

"Yeah, I have experience." Pensive, she stared off toward the activities on the green. The dogs busily sniffed around the sidewalk, pulling at their leashes, and she absently pulled them back. "Too bad about that Gary Booker." She shrugged. "But what goes around comes around, I guess."

Before Shannon could ask what she meant by that cryptic remark, the dogs tugged again and she was gone, all her energy focused on not letting them run into the street.

Inside, the store was jammed with customers standing three deep at the register. Upon spotting Shannon, Essie's face sagged in relief. "I was hoping you'd get here soon," she said as Shannon slipped behind the counter to help.

"Where's Carrie?" Shannon asked.

Essie shook her head with a look of disgust. "She called in sick again. I don't know what's wrong with her. I was too busy to ask, so I called the twins. They'll be here any minute."

"Good. I'll go see Carrie after the store closes." As Shannon placed purchases in a bag, she wondered what was going on with her employee. She had always been reliable. *Until Gary Booker came along.*

When the twins arrived, they informed Shannon that the big tree had been put up in the mansion entryway and was ready for decorating. "Maybe when we're not busy here, we could pick out a new ornament to commemorate this Christmas?" Lara asked hopefully. "I saw some really pretty ones the artists made when Alec and I decorated here the other day."

"That's a nice idea," Shannon said. "You two work in the coffee shop, OK?"

The afternoon passed quickly with craft supplies and gifts flying off the shelves. Shannon sold the last of her silver Madonna and Child pendants and most of her Star of Bethlehem pins. As the time drew closer for the tree lighting, patrons purchased large hot chocolates and coffees to go. Carrie's concoctions were a big hit, and again Shannon wondered at her out-of-character behavior. She hoped there wasn't a sinister reason for her absence.

At ten to six, Lara and Alec asked if they could go to the tree-lighting ceremony. "Why don't you all go?" Essie suggested. "I'll close up."

"Are you sure?" Shannon asked. "It's been a busy day; you must be tired."

"Of course I'm sure. You bought a star for John. You really need to be there."

"Please come with us, Mum," Lara pleaded. "We can always clean up later."

"Good idea. Essie, you cash out and lock up. We'll take care of the rest. The Purls are having a special meeting tonight, so I have to come back anyway." At Essie's protests, Shannon held up her hand. "You've done enough. Enjoy your day off tomorrow." *Essie looks tired*, Shannon reflected. Dark circles under her eyes marred her pretty face, and her cheeks were pale. She'd been carrying more than her share of the load lately. Maybe the twins should take more hours, at least until Christmas.

"I might come in tomorrow afternoon and help restock," Essie said. "A bunch of shipments are scheduled to come in."

"Only if you feel like it," Shannon said. "Honestly, I can handle it."

As they walked toward the green, Shannon noticed Hillary was helping Chaz sell trees. He needed the help; even as she watched, trees were purchased and loaded onto vehicles. Clusters of people were scattered around the green, which still had traces of snow here and there. In town, the temperatures were slightly warmer than at the farm. Shannon and the twins worked their way through the crowd, getting as close to the big tree as they could. All around them, families laughed and chatted, white plumes of breath mingling in the frosty air.

"Where's our star, Mum?" Lara asked.

"I have no idea. There are hundreds." Holding hands, the three of them gazed up at the enormous, ancient fir, standing proudly against a backdrop of star-filled sky. The buildings and streets surrounding the green were cheerful with Christmas lights and decorations glowing.

Pastor Boyer took the podium set up to one side of the

tree. "I'd like to welcome you all to Apple Grove tonight. It's great to see such a large turnout of residents and visitors. This year, we exceeded our goal for the fundraiser." Everyone cheered. "That means those in need will have a brighter Christmas, thanks to your generosity." Cheers again. The pastor led a brief prayer of dedication and blessing upon the Christmas season and those in need. Bowing her head along with everyone else, Shannon thought how beautiful it was to bring people together to bless others.

"And now, the moment we've all been waiting for," he said at the conclusion of the prayer. He waved his hand to the unseen person holding the power switch.

The colored lights on the tree sprang to life, eliciting oohs and aahs from the crowd. Here and there, the metal star ornaments caught the light, twinkling as they swayed in the light evening breeze. Shannon squeezed the kids' hands, knowing they were thinking of their father, as she was.

"I miss Daddy," Lara whispered. "But I'm OK about it now. It doesn't hurt so much to think about him."

Alec kissed Shannon on the cheek. "Love you, Mum. Thanks for making such a great home for us here," he said, pointing to the sky. "We'll see Dad again someday."

Releasing their hands, Shannon brushed tears away. "Stop it, you two. You'll have me bawling like a babe."

The church choir, dressed in Victorian garb including long skirts, tailcoats, top hats, and fur-trimmed muffs, stepped forward and began to sing carols. At the edge of the green, a food van benefiting the Boy and Girl Scouts opened for business, offering hot dogs, sausages, pizza, and other mouthwatering delights.

"You two grab something to eat before you go back to the store," Shannon urged, handing them cash. "Get me a slice of pizza. I have to go see Carrie and make sure she's OK. If the Purls show up before I do, tell them I'll be right back and to make themselves at home." She thought of something she'd been putting off. "Oh, and before I forget, can you please call Chief Grayson at the station tomorrow morning and tell him what you saw yesterday out at the farm?"

Lara and Alec looked at each other. "I didn't see anything except trees and snowmen," Alec said, referring to the signposts.

"Yeah," Lara chimed in. "Those were so cute. They had real hats."

Shannon felt relieved. The twins hadn't seen anything Grayson would need beyond their initial statement. At least they wouldn't be involved in the investigation, which was more than she could say for herself.

— 13 —

Carrie lived on a side street near the green, in one of the rambling, proud old houses that had been made over into apartments. Number five was in the rear with its own entrance and a nice-size yard right outside the door. Several cars were parked in the drive, but Shannon didn't know which one belonged to Carrie since the girl always walked to work.

None of the lights were on, and as Shannon knocked on the glass of the door, she wondered if Carrie was in bed or even at home. Calls had gone right to voice mail. Curtains blocked her view, but through a little crack, she could see the edge of a stove and refrigerator in the light given off by the stove's digital display.

Shannon was starting to worry. Essie had said Carrie sounded ill, her voice merely a hoarse mumble. For a moment, her imagination went wild and she pictured Carrie hurt and afraid to go to the police. What if Finn had beat her up? Or what if they were in on the murder together, and Carrie was lying low?

She knocked again, louder this time, and then waited, wondering what to do. The last thing she wanted was to call the police in for a false alarm. She was just ready to pull out her cellphone anyway when she heard footsteps shuffling toward the door. The curtain twitched aside, and then Shannon heard the lock rattle.

The door creaked open slowly. Carrie stood there, wearing baggy flannel pajamas, her hair a snarled tangle, her eyes and nose red and swollen. "Shannon," she said, her voice scratchy. "What are you doing here?"

"May I come in?" Shannon asked, entering the apartment when Carrie stood back and opened the door a little wider. "I was worried about you. You didn't answer the phone, so I thought I'd come check on you. Make sure you're OK."

"Thanks. That's nice of you." Carrie shuffled her way into the next room, a small, sparsely furnished living room illuminated only by one small lamp. A rumpled crocheted afghan on the sofa, heaps of balled-up tissues, and drawn drapes told the story. It appeared Carrie had been holed up, mourning Gary's death. *Or is she hiding from her own guilt?*

Besides the sofa and a matching overstuffed chair, the room held little furniture. On the fireplace mantel stood a line of sporting trophies, many with ribbons and medals hanging around them. "Have a seat," Carrie said, collapsing again on the sofa.

Instead, Shannon moved to the trophies, interested to learn more about Carrie. Often it was better to break the ice with neutral topics rather than jump right into the difficult questions.

"Did you grow up around here?" Shannon asked. Betty had said so, but she didn't want Carrie to know she'd been discussed.

"Yeah. Lived here my whole life, except when I went to college. Afterward, I decided to come back."

"Do you still have family around?" Perhaps someone could come over and stay with her.

Carrie shook her head. Picking up a tissue, she blew her nose. "Nope. My dad died while I was in college."

Shannon felt a pang. That was tough, she knew, having gone through it with the twins. "And your mom?"

"My mother moved to Seattle with her new husband several years ago. I get up there once or twice a year." She tried to smile. "You'd realize that's often enough if you knew my mother."

Shannon changed the subject. "I see you played a lot of sports. I didn't know that about you." Most of the trophies were for golf and tennis, but one had a Diana the Huntress figure. Archery. Another had a female figure sighting a rifle. Among the ribbons was one with a circular motif that looked familiar. Where had she seen something like that?

Carrie coughed. "I still play tennis and golf."

Shannon settled on the chair. "I get the feeling that you're more upset about Gary than actually sick," she said gently.

Tears filled Carrie's eyes, and she ducked her head quickly to hide them. "You'd think there wouldn't be an ounce of water in my body, I've cried so much." With an effort, she got her tears under control and said, "You're right. I'm not really sick. I suppose you'd be justified in firing me."

"I'm not going to fire you. I understand how hard it is to lose someone you care about. Just because you weren't married doesn't mean it's not devastating."

"Thanks for understanding. Most people would think I'm overreacting, since we just started dating. But I really loved Gary." Carrie stared down at the afghan, her fingers plucking at a loose strand of yarn. "I tried not to. Love him, that is. He was a liar and a cheat." She made a horrific attempt to laugh. "No woman was safe around him."

She was silent, tugging away at the wool. "You must think I'm crazy to even date someone like that. But he had a way of making you feel like you were beautiful and exciting."

"That can be addictive," Shannon said. She herself knew how Michael just entering the room gave everything a special luster. What if he wasn't an honest and upright individual? Would the thrill be worth the possible letdown? She was thankful she didn't have to wonder about the answer to that.

"The worst thing," Carrie said tentatively, "is that we actually broke up before he … ah, um … you know. We had a big fight, and I told him if he couldn't stop hitting on other girls, I couldn't see him anymore."

"Was that the night you had dinner at the inn?"

"Oh, did Betty tell you about the scene I made?" Carrie squirmed. "I'm so embarrassed."

"Don't be. It sounds like Gary was being a jerk." Shannon hesitated and then asked, "So that was the last time you saw him?"

"Yes. The very last time." Carrie squirmed again, her eyes not meeting Shannon's, and Shannon wondered if she was lying. Tears gushed from Carrie's eyes. "I was so hateful to him! And now he'll never know how I really feel."

Shannon found a few fresh tissues and handed them to Carrie. "He knows, Carrie. I'm sure of that." *Poor girl*, she thought, *worried about letting down a philandering jerk*. He hadn't deserved her devotion, that was certain. "Where was Gary from? I had the sense he wasn't local."

"He moved up here about a year and a half ago. From Pine Valley, he said. That's somewhere down south."

"His family must be devastated too," Shannon murmured, quite frankly fishing for information.

"Gary didn't have any family. Both his parents are dead. That's something else we bonded over. Well, my mother is still alive, but she might as well be dead for all the attention I get."

Shannon wondered how to broach the topic of Finn. She didn't want to admit she knew they had dated in high school, again fearing to appear a snoop.

Finally she decided to just say it. "While I was at the Olsons' today, Finn said he came to see you yesterday."

Carrie's eyes widened in shock, and Shannon could see her turn over various responses in her mind. "He said that? Huh."

She said nothing else, so Shannon upped the ante a bit to encourage another response. "Yes, that's what he told the police." Shannon felt a qualm of misgiving. What if she was messing up the chief's evidence gathering? Oh well, it was too late now. "I was just surprised because I didn't know you knew each other."

"We dated in high school," Carrie admitted. "We used to fish and hunt together, believe it or not." Her face turned red. "He was here, but that's all I have to say about it, OK?"

She was hiding something.

"Of course," Shannon said. "Whatever happened between you and Finn is none of my business." Shannon noticed that Carrie's face reddened further. "Just be sure to tell the police he was here when they ask, OK? Don't lie. It could be really important."

"Is Finn a suspect? Oh no!" Carrie put both hands to

her mouth and stared into the distance like she was seeing something truly terrifying.

Gosh, she had really put her foot in it. "Not that I know of," Shannon lied. "The police like to get everyone's alibi, that's all. They'll probably ask you too, since people knew you were dating Gary."

Carrie gasped. "Are they coming here?" She looked around frantically. "This place is a mess! *I'm* a mess!"

Shannon put her hands on Carrie's shoulders. "Calm down. Everything will be all right. Just tell the truth. Look, the store is closed tomorrow, but we'll be doing restocking. Come over if you feel up to it, OK?"

"You really mean I'm not fired? Thanks—you won't regret this. I really love working at the store, you know. I'll be there tomorrow."

"I know. And by the way, everyone just loves your hot chocolate combos. So think up a new one."

"I will." Carrie followed Shannon to the door, continuing to murmur reassurances about her commitment to the store.

Walking back to the market, Shannon reflected on what she had learned about Gary's background and the relationship between Finn and Carrie.

I hope whatever Finn and Carrie are up to, it's not criminal.

She went by the green, deserted now except for the glowing, giant tree. The food truck was closed up, and while she watched, it drove away. Her cellphone rang, a jarring noise in the quiet night. When she dug it out of her bag, her heart lifted. It was Michael.

"Hello," she caroled. "How was the rest of your day?"

"I've got good news and bad news." He paused dramatically.

"Go on, spill!"

"The good news is I got a new client today."

"That's super. A big job, I hope." She knew Michael preferred to take on fewer but larger jobs rather than multiple small ones, as they were easier to implement and monitor.

"Oh yes. Huge. The bad news is, I have to go out of town. Tonight."

Now her heart sank. "Tonight?"

"Yeah." His tone was glum. "I hope I'll be back in time for Christmas."

She stopped dead in the street, biting back a shriek. He couldn't be out of town on Christmas! It would ruin everything. "Oh, Michael," she said when she could trust herself to speak. This was worse for him, she reminded herself. She at least had the twins and Beth and her friends to spend Christmas with.

He gave a great, heartrending sigh. "I was so tempted to say no, but it will really make a big difference to my company. The CEO promised me that if we do a good job on the Tokyo assignment, we'll get a five-year contract for their northwestern U.S. work. That means Seattle and Portland. The contract will include an overseas manager, so I won't have to travel much at all."

"You have to go, then," she said firmly. "We'll have our own Christmas when you get back. And God willing, you'll make it home by December twenty-fifth."

"Thanks. That means a lot to me. I'll make it up to you, I promise."

"Just get back here safely. That's all I want."

"And you be careful with whatever you get into with Booker's death. I have a feeling it could get nasty."

— 14 —

When Shannon got back to the store, she found Betty, Melanie, and Joyce working on the hats and mittens for the Angel Tree. "The twins went home, but they left you a piece of pizza," Joyce said, working on a bright pink hat. "And I brought my mince pie samples for dessert."

Shannon eyed the tray of mince tarts topped with star-shaped pastry cutouts as she put the pizza slice into the microwave. "They look great."

"They taste as good as they look," Melanie said. "I can vouch for that!"

Shannon took a bite of tart. One of the perks of being an adult was eating dessert first, right? "Oh my. This is perfect. Not too sweet. And the pastry just melts in your mouth."

Joyce smiled smugly. "Thanks for the official seal of approval. They'll be Day Five of my Twelve Days of Christmas Cookies. Did I mention that I'm doing an international theme? So far, I have traditional recipes for Mexico, Norway, Germany, and now, Scotland."

"That sounds incredible, Joyce," Melanie said.

"How is Carrie?" Betty asked Shannon. "Lara said you went to see her."

The microwave dinged and Shannon brought her meal to a small table near the circle of chairs. "She's pretty upset," she said. "She really cared about that bounder."

"I'm sure we all have a bad boy in our past," Joyce remarked. "They can be pretty irresistible."

"Is Kate coming tonight?" Before Shannon finished the question, the door to the shop jangled.

"Sounds like she's here," Betty said.

Kate and Jake Stager entered the coffee shop, arm in arm. Kate's cheeks were glowing and she smiled radiantly. "Does everyone know Jake?" she asked, proceeding to introduce him.

"I saw your article," Betty said. "Nice job."

He scuffed the toe of his leather boot on the tile floor, looking both pleased and abashed. "Thanks. I'm trying to get more meaty assignments. Not that covering Apple Grove's Christmas celebration isn't great," he added hastily.

"I saw you at the tree lighting," Melanie said. "It was so gorgeous!" Making a funny face, she added, "I even put a star on the tree for Edward."

The others oohed in surprise. Edward, murdered and buried on the site of the coffee shop, had been Melanie's cheating ex-husband.

"You're amazing, girl," Joyce said frankly.

Melanie shrugged. "Even though he was a jerk, he didn't deserve to be murdered. Maybe he's seen the error of his ways."

"Forgiveness is a beautiful thing," Betty commented. "So, Kate, are you staying with us tonight?"

"Yes," Kate said. "Jake wanted to get a coffee, and then he's going over to the pub to watch the dart league and wait for me." She smiled fondly at Jake, who beamed back.

Jake patted his coat chest pocket. "I might throw a few myself. Brought my best darts, just in case."

Shannon got up from the table, carrying her empty plate. "I'll fix you a coffee, Jake. Anyone else?"

Kate found her knitting project in the basket and sat with the others, and Jake joined Shannon at the counter. While she poured him a tall take-out cup, he leaned forward. "I heard the police were out at the farm again," he said quietly. "Any chance Booker's death was a murder?"

Yes.

Shannon shook her head, adding cream to her own cup. "I really can't talk about it right now. It's up to the chief to release new information."

"I understand," he said, stirring sugar into his coffee. He put the cap on and lifted the cup. "What do I owe you?"

"On the house. A friend of Kate's is a friend of mine." She leaned forward. "When and if I have anything I can say, I promise I'll come to you first. OK, Jake?"

"Fair enough. I appreciate it." He raised his voice to include the room. "Good night, ladies." He pointed at Kate. "I'll see *you* later!"

Kate giggled merrily. "I'll meet you at the pub after we finish up."

As the jingle of bells announced Jake's departure, Melanie said slyly, "I see you have a new friend."

Kate blushed furiously and stared down at the hat she was knitting. "Yes, I guess I do. He's wonderful."

"I can tell," Betty said. "He only has eyes for you."

"That's how it should be," Joyce said in her usual outspoken style. Tonight she wore a lovely pink silk blouse under a matching cashmere sweater. Her bright, inquisitive eyes landed on Shannon. "Speaking of wonderful men, how's Michael?"

Despite an effort to appear chipper, Shannon felt her face fall. "He's going out of town and may not be back until after Christmas." She stared down at the soft white mittens she was knitting. A lucky little girl would love them.

The others protested loudly. "What kind of client would do that?" Joyce cried.

"He's going to Japan. I guess Christmas isn't exactly a priority over there." Shannon shrugged. "It's an important job for his company. Maybe a five-year contract."

"That is a plum assignment these days," Melanie said.

"I'll pray that he's back in time," Betty said stoutly. "Families need to be together on Christmas."

Shannon felt herself flush at the notion of Michael as family. She was beginning to admit to herself that she hoped he might officially become that someday. "Thanks, Betty," she murmured.

"Speaking of family," Kate said, "how about adopting Boyd? I haven't been able to find his owner."

"That fluffy blond dog Shannon found?" Melanie asked. "Who named him?"

"Shannon. It means 'yellow' in Gaelic, right, Shannon?" Kate bound off the top of the blue hat she was knitting. "Another one done."

"Someone said to name something is to own it," Joyce suggested slyly.

"I don't know about having a pet," Shannon said. "I'm so busy here."

"Think about it, OK?" Kate said. "He really seems to love you."

*   *   *

Shannon woke the next day to brilliant sunshine and the sound of melting snow dripping off the eaves. In the distance, the ocean was calm and blue, a serene reflection of the overarching dome of cloudless sky. According to the forecast, today would be warm enough to work outdoors on her jewelry. But first she and the twins had something important to do: decorate the big tree.

"Look at this, Mum," Lara squealed, holding up a tiny white vintage hatbox ornament before dropping it into the palm of Shannon's hand. "It must be a hundred years old."

Lara and Shannon were unpacking Victoria's Christmas ornaments while Alec wrestled with wrapping long strings of lights around the huge tree. Fortunately, they had found a stepladder tall enough for him to reach the highest branches without endangering life and limb.

Shannon peered at the hatbox. "Oh my. It has a real little hat inside!" she exclaimed in delight.

"This whole series must represent a lady's wardrobe," Lara said. She displayed one ornament after another. "A parasol, dressmaker dummy, and itsy-bitsy shoes."

"I like the sailboat ornaments," Alec said from his position on the ladder. "And the sports ones." He was referring to a very old set consisting of a hockey stick, skis, sled, and skates. All the pieces were made of carved and painted wood. "Grandmother Victoria sure must have liked collecting ornaments. There must be thousands of them." Holding up the plug at the end of a string, he called, "Hey, Lara, hand me the next set."

Lara jumped up and handed Alec another string of lights. Shannon continued to work her way through the tubs, taking out cardboard boxes of ornaments and peeking inside. In addition to traditional glass balls and teardrops, many were Victorian themed. The materials were unusual— brass mesh, paper, silk, and beads, even feathers. Santas and elves and angels.

Angels. Shannon opened a box holding three handblown glass angels. They were so delicate and fragile, it seemed a breath might shatter them. One held a trumpet; the second, a flute; and the third, a lute. The workmanship was precise and exquisite, each angel rendered in great detail and paint-ed in soft colors trimmed with gold. An empty slot revealed that one in the set was missing.

"Lara! Alec!" she cried. They came running over, and wordlessly, she showed them the box. Lara gasped. She went to the box that held the Christmas decorations they had brought from Scotland, their most cherished collection. It included heirlooms from John's family, ornaments hand-made by the twins, and one special item. Lara found what she was looking for—a small white box—and hurried back. Opening the box, she unwrapped an ornament from its co-coon of white cotton and held it gently in her hand.

An angel playing a harp. It perfectly matched the set.

"Beth gave you this, didn't she?" Lara said.

Shannon nodded. She remembered the first and only Christmas she had been old enough to help Beth trim the tree. Beth had told her the ornament had been her favorite as a little girl and now it was to be Shannon's. Each year, with mingled love and pain, Shannon had placed that ornament in a prominent spot on the Christmas tree. It was a link to the mother who had so tenderly explained the miracle of angels announcing the newborn King in the skies over Bethlehem.

"I've got an idea," Lara said. She carefully placed the angel in its slot next to its fellows. Then she pulled out her phone and took a picture of all four.

"What are you doing?" Alec asked, bemused. "Putting the angels on your Facebook page?"

"No. Sending Grandmother Beth a text. See?" She showed Shannon and Alec her phone. The message "Home again" was written under the photo. She quickly pushed the button and a *whoosh* sound announced the message's departure.

"Does Beth text?" Shannon asked, amused.

Lara nodded. "Of course." Immediately, her phone dinged, announcing a reply. She showed them Beth's message: "Can't wait to see all four angels together on the tree again. Love you."

"Four angels. The four of us. Nice symmetry to that," Alec mused. "Come on, let's get the rest of the lights on."

*   *   *

Since a good part of the silver-and-enamel jewelry-making process required a torch and kiln, Shannon preferred to work in a shed behind the Paisley Craft Market. The main market building was old and wooden, and she didn't want to risk a fire. In addition, soldering gave off fumes, and she could leave the shed's sliding door wide open to the fresh air.

As Shannon unlocked the padlock securing the shed, she reflected on the progression of her jewelry art. She'd

started with beadwork, added silversmithing, and now had
been trained in enameling. Each technique gave her fresh
inspiration along with new skills in working with precious
metals, glass, and jewels.

Hammered silver bases for her Madonna and Child
pendants awaited on the long workbench. Shannon fired up
the kiln, and while waiting for it to reach the right temperature, she glued thin strands of gold wire to the pendants.
These would hold the enamel powder in place during firing,
keeping the colors separate. *The Nutcracker Suite* played
on the old radio she kept in here, broadcast by the classical
station, and close at hand were fresh cranberry scones and a
big, insulated mug of coffee she'd brought from home.

"Hi, Shannon," Essie said, appearing in the shed doorway. She glanced at her watch, a beaded confection pinned
to her cowl-neck sweater shawl. "UPS will be here any minute with that big shipment." She peered at Shannon's work.
"Can I look?"

"Sure." Shannon stood back while Essie examined the
rich blue enamel she was applying to highlight the curves of
Mary's arms, cradling the baby within their protection. Gold
halos circled both heads.

"Wow." She patted her heart. "Those get me every time.
Just gorgeous."

"Thanks. Me too. There's something special about making Christmas jewelry. A little extra love and meaning in the
work. At least that's what I always feel."

"It comes through, believe me. I want to wear one on
Christmas Eve."

"I'll make you one. My gift." Shannon put up a hand

to forestall Essie's protests. "And it won't come out of your Christmas bonus. I couldn't run this place without you, Essie. I mean that."

Essie's cheeks pinked, but her smile was wide. "That's so nice to hear. I love working here, and I'm glad you think I'm doing a good job."

"Well, you are." Shannon picked up her brush and dipped it into enamel powder. She needed to add another layer of blue. "By the way, I went to see Carrie last night, and she's coming in to help you this afternoon."

Essie's smile faded. "How is she?"

"OK. Upset over Gary, of course."

Essie's voice was brisk. "Good. I'll have tons for her to do." Her tone suggested that she wasn't as forgiving as Shannon about Carrie's two-day defection since she hadn't actually been physically ill. Moving to the doorway, she said, "I'd better get inside before the truck comes."

"One more thing," Shannon said, setting down her brush. She opened her purse and pulled a twenty-dollar bill out of her wallet. "How about getting sandwiches for all of us for lunch? You can leave mine on my desk. I'll be in when I reach a good stopping point."

After a few hours of enameling, Shannon cleaned up her tools and went inside the market to do paperwork. Since the store was closed on Mondays, she often spent the day paying bills and entering transactions into the computer. But before starting her tasks, she unwrapped the still-warm turkey-and-artichoke panini Essie had left on her desk and took a bite. Yum. Making jewelry in the fresh air had given her an appetite.

From out in the shop came the murmur of voices as Essie and Carrie stocked shelves and rearranged displays. While Shannon liked to keep product categories in the same general area to make shopping easy for repeat customers, sales were often boosted by putting new or slow-to-sell items in a prominent position. Both Essie and Carrie were talented at making displays look interesting and attractive.

Someone rapped on the front door, apparently ignoring the "Closed" sign. A moment later, she heard Betty ask, "Is Shannon here?" The distress and concern in her voice were palpable, so Shannon abandoned her sandwich and went out to see what was wrong. Betty stood just inside the doorway, her normally neat hair windblown. She appeared breathless, as though she'd been running. Essie shut and relocked the door while Carrie watched, frozen in her task of restocking colorful wool yarn in cubbies.

"What's the matter, Betty?" Shannon asked, her heart beating faster. "Are Tom and the kids all right?" *It must be something bad, or Betty would simply have called.*

Betty flapped her hand. "Oh, they're fine. It's Finn Olson. Chief Grayson has arrested him for murder."

— 15 —

"**F**inn's been arrested?" Shannon shook her head in dismay, her heart aching with sympathy for the Olsons. "Poor Marge and Dick. This will destroy them."

"Oh!" came a gasp. Shannon and the others turned to see Carrie slump to the floor. She collapsed into a tight ball, hugging her knees and rocking.

"Essie, get me one of the afghans, please." Shannon ran to Carrie's side, crouching down next to her. Betty followed and knelt on Carrie's other side.

"Finn shot Gary? No!" Carrie began to wail, rocking harder. "It's all my fault!"

Shannon and Betty exchanged looks. Essie handed Shannon the blanket, and she draped it around Carrie's shoulders. "Come on, Carrie, get up." It took some urging, but eventually they were able to coax the stunned young woman to get up and move to one of the leather chairs in the coffee shop. Once there, she slumped back, both hands over her face, muttering low cries of disbelief.

"How about some hot chocolate, Essie?" Shannon suggested.

"I could use some," Betty said, sinking down into a chair. "This whole thing is a nightmare."

"If he's innocent," Essie agreed, going behind the counter, "then yes, it is." Essie had been a suspect in a murder, and she knew firsthand the world-shattering dismay and terror involved. She pulled out four mugs and began to mix hot chocolate.

"What evidence do they have?" Shannon asked Betty quietly. As far as she knew, the only evidence was opportunity and Finn's inability to establish an alibi. Had the police questioned Carrie? Looking at her distraught figure, she doubted it was a good time to inquire.

"They got a warrant for Finn's hunting equipment, and two arrows were missing. I heard they discovered the shooter was on farm property. That's all I know."

"I decided to make us all the Naughty," Essie said, referring to the double-chocolate drink Carrie had invented. She passed out big mugs topped with lots of whipped cream. "I figured today's news calls for an extra-big blast of chocolate."

Shannon perched on a stool to drink her hot chocolate while keeping an eye on Carrie and thinking about the new developments. Finn did have a horrendous temper, no doubt about it. He and Gary had been in two fistfights that she knew about. He also disliked Gary for what he considered his pernicious influence on his parents. "Unfortunately, Finn is a bow hunter," Shannon commented, picking up the thread of the conversation. "I'm sure that's a very limited pool."

"Even if Finn is a very good hunter with excellent aim," Betty observed, "wouldn't he have covered his tracks better?"

"True," Shannon agreed. It would be pretty careless to leave evidence on your own property. Carrie had stopped moaning and was sitting with her eyes closed, both hands clasping the warm mug of cocoa. Despite her apparent inattention, Shannon sensed she was listening very closely. "Let's go see Marge and Dick and talk to them about it."

If Finn were innocent, then either someone had shot Gary in passion or had tried to frame Finn. Or both. That person needed to have access to Finn's equipment. Carrie, despite her apparent shock and distress, fell into that category.

*　　*　　*

Betty drove out to the farm, and Shannon was glad to watch the rolling countryside while gathering her thoughts. Finn's arrest was her fault. If she and Michael had left things alone, the police might have chalked up Gary's death to an unfortunate accident. On the other hand, justice needed to be served. So why did this particular outcome feel so wrong?

"My heart absolutely aches for the Olsons," Betty said. "They've just gotten Finn back home and this happens." She set her jaw firmly. "I don't believe Finn did it. I'll never believe that."

"Finn and Gary did have a couple of fights," Shannon reminded her. "Remember the first time we came out here? And the night of the wreath class, Gary's lip was swollen."

"Maybe so," Betty said. "But murder?" She snorted. "Finn is just like Dick; his bark is far worse than his bite."

Shannon hoped she was right.

At the farmhouse, Marge was in the living room, sitting in front of a fire that was roaring in the massive stone fireplace. Dick was lying down in the room across the hall. Due to his broken leg, he couldn't climb stairs, and a bed had been set up in there.

"I just can't get warm," Marge said. She sat with a crocheted throw around her shoulders, her wing chair drawn up close to the hearth. She rubbed her arms with both hands, teeth chattering. "My head is spinning with it all."

"We can understand that," Betty said gently. She and Shannon took seats on the low-backed antique sofa upholstered in green shadow-stripe silk. Like the sofa, the rest of the room reflected the Olson family's long history on the property. A faded black-and-white photograph on the mantel showed the newly built house and barn, men and women in old-fashioned garb standing on the porch. A secretary-style cabinet displayed a porcelain shepherd and shepherdess, willowware plates, and a silver teapot.

Marge followed Shannon's gaze to the collection. "All that was brought west by Dick's great-great-grandparents," Marge said. "They settled this land in the mid-1800s." Her voice cracked. "Who knows what will happen to it now?"

A light tap sounded on the half-open door. "Come in," Marge called. Hillary entered, hefting a large tray laden with a teapot, cups, plates, and a platter of chocolate-chip cookies. While they watched in silence, she carefully set it on the marble-topped coffee table in front of Betty and Shannon.

"All settled in?" Shannon asked her.

Hillary jumped. "Oh, are you talking to me? Yes, everything is great." She cast a nervous glance at Marge. "Is this all right, Mrs. Olson? I followed your instructions when I made the tea."

Marge didn't even turn her head. "I'm sure it's fine. Thank you, Hillary."

"I'm going to go load trees then," she said, quickly exiting. "Call if you need anything. I'll be right outside."

Betty poured tea, giving the first cup to their hostess.

"That girl is a godsend," Marge said with a sigh. "She knows her way around a tree farm, that's for sure." She

stared into the fire, her lips working. Then, with sudden re-
solve, she put the cup and saucer down on a side table with
a clatter. "I can't imagine what you think of us. We must
look a right mess."

"I wouldn't say that." Shannon picked up a cookie and
bit into it. It was made with butter, she could tell. Butter
made all the difference in the texture and taste of a cookie.

Now that she had decided to unburden herself, Marge
wouldn't be put off. "Well, you might be justified in thinking that. We made a lot of mistakes with Finn when he was
a boy. Dick insisted that he take over the farm, and Finn
didn't want to. That's happening everywhere, you know.
Young'uns get their fill of farming as children and run off as
fast as they can. Who can blame them? It's a hard life." She
sighed, wringing her worn and reddened hands that testified
to her words. "But it means everything to Dick to keep this
place going. So when Gary Booker came along and took an
interest, helped us out, well, I guess we made him a surrogate son. We even—" She halted.

Shannon waited breathlessly for her to continue. Betty,
too, was on the edge of her seat.

Marge swallowed hard. "We even put him in the will."
Her voice was merely a hoarse croak.

Shannon's heart sank. Talk about a strong motive for
Finn to kill Gary.

"Did Finn know that?" Betty asked.

Marge's face crumpled. "Yes. That night he fought with
Gary and then took off, he had searched the office and
found the paperwork. After he found out about the subdivision plans, that led him to dig deeper, I guess."

For a moment, the clock ticking on the mantel and the snap and crackle of a settling log were the only sounds in the room. Shannon reflected on it all. The prodigal son and the surrogate. The Olsons, striving to maintain a hundred-year legacy of land and farming. Betrayal. Murder.

"Marge," she asked, "when you changed the will, did you think Finn would ever be back?"

"No," she replied. "Never. Of course we heard from him now and then, but he made it plain he wanted nothing to do with the farm. And we finally accepted that."

"So why did he come back now? Was there a reason, or was it just a holiday visit?" Shannon felt her heart beat a little faster. Somehow she sensed the answer to this question was important, a missing piece to the story of what had happened and why.

"No, it wasn't a holiday visit." Marge's tone was wry. "Someone wrote to him and warned him Gary was taking over the farm."

"Who?" Betty asked, her jaw dropping. "Who would do a thing like that?"

"We don't know. It was an anonymous email, Finn said. He wouldn't have believed it, but they had included a link to the planning board's minutes of the meeting when we went in for the subdivision."

Shannon remembered Carrie saying it was her fault. Could she have sent the email? But surely she wouldn't have upset Gary's applecart that way.

In an odd echo of her thoughts, Marge said, "It's all our fault. We handled everything wrong. Finn. Gary. The property issue. And now our son's going to jail for life."

"It's not over yet," Betty said firmly. "I don't believe Finn is guilty. Don't be so hard on yourself. You and Dick were doing the best you could in a tough situation."

"You are too kind," Marge said. "Your friendship means more than you know." She looked at Shannon. "Yours, too, Shannon dear."

"I've been thinking," Shannon said.

"Yes?" Marge's gaze was curious.

Shannon hesitated, wrestling with the wisdom of what she was about to say. The case against Finn looked pretty clear-cut. However, in her view, the anonymous message shed enough doubt to call for further investigation. But what if she was wrong and Finn was guilty? Was it fair to arouse false hope? Taking a deep breath, she plunged ahead. "I'm going to look into a few things, if that's all right with you."

"What do you mean?"

"Shannon has solved a lot of murders," Betty explained. "She has quite a knack for it."

"So you can get Finn off the hook?"

Shannon took a deep breath. "I can't promise anything. Whatever I find, whoever it implicates, I'll have to take the evidence to the police."

"Fine. I know he's innocent, so please, go ahead. Let's find out who did this horrible thing and pinned the blame on my son."

Shannon realized with a sinking feeling that of course, all parents think their children are innocent. She hoped that's what she would end up discovering.

"I'm not saying that just because he's my son," Marge continued in defiance of Shannon's conclusion. "Finn is too

smart to leave evidence around here. If he wanted to murder someone, he would have covered it up better."

It was an interesting argument for the defense, one that Betty
had also made. Both claimed he was too smart to incriminate himself. Shannon fervently hoped they were right, for the Olsons' sake.

"So what do you do when you investigate?" Marge asked.

Shannon rummaged around in her bag and pulled out a
notepad and pen. "The first thing I like to do is learn more
about the victim. I'd like to ask you a few questions if you're
up for it. Then I want to take a look at Gary's room."

"The police have been all through it. They took his cellphone, I know that. What are you looking for?"

"Anything that will help me understand Gary better.
Any clues to his past life." Shannon let Marge think about
that for a moment, then asked, "Would you like me to start
now, or should I come back later?"

"Let's do it now. The sooner we solve this, the sooner
Finn can come home."

Shannon led Marge through a series of questions regarding Gary's arrival and background. He'd appeared a year and a
half ago, claiming that someone in Apple Grove had said they
needed help, which was true. Marge wasn't exactly sure where
he was from—somewhere in southern Oregon, she thought.
Gary didn't like talking about his past, and she didn't like prob-
ing. She was under the impression that he had no family.

"What about a vehicle?" Shannon asked. "He didn't arrive on foot, did he?"

"He had an old beater truck on its last legs. He sold it
after he was here a while. We let him use the farm truck and
van whenever he wanted, of course."

"Do you know who bought it?"

Marge shook her head. "He put an ad on that Craigslist thing. Guy showed up, bought it, and drove it away."

Probably a dead end there, which was too bad, as the old registration would give an address. "Did he give you any references or information about past employment?"

Marge's face reddened. "That's what Finn wanted to know. We didn't ask, I'm ashamed to say. We could tell he knew what he was doing around the farm, and that was good enough for us. He told us his last employer had died." Standing up with a slight groan, Marge threw another log on the fire and nudged it into place with a poker. "Gary helped us a lot, you know. He was always studying up on how to make the farm more profitable."

Shannon closed her notepad. "I think we're all set for now. I'd like to take a look at his room." With any luck, she would discover more about the elusive and mysterious Gary Booker among his belongings.

Marge gave Shannon the key, and she and Betty went up to search Gary's room. He and the other workers had bedrooms in a wing of the farmhouse reached by stairs in the laundry room, which was off the kitchen. This part of the house was more rustic, with creaky, wide-board wooden floors and plain plaster walls.

"It looks like this part of the house has always been used by hired help," Betty whispered as they walked down the dim hall to Gary's room. He had been assigned the fourth and final room in the wing. Shannon turned the big, old-fashioned brass key in the lock and opened the door.

Although the rectangular room was small and furnished

only with a single bed, chest of drawers, and an armchair, it boasted two windows, one overlooking the trees and the other, the barn. Hooks in one corner served as a closet, and a wall shelf held a long line of books. Everything was neat and in good order. Even the bed was made, an old-fashioned tufted chenille spread pulled over the pillows.

Shannon squashed her discomfort at invading Gary's personal space and stepped into the room. This was a necessary step in discovering his killer, she told herself.

Unless Finn was guilty, of course.

"Look through the books, Betty. I'll check the dresser."

"I guess he did study farming a lot," Betty commented as she took each book off the shelf and shook it. "He has books on making your farm profitable, tree diseases, propagation, you name it."

Like many men, Gary had had a habit of storing loose items on top of his bureau, and he'd used a carved wooden bowl to hold his odds and ends. Shannon dug through it first. The contents included coins, a pen, coupons for local restaurants, extra keys, a tiny jackknife, and a book of matches. The jacket of the matches read "Miss Oregon Diner, Pine Valley, OR." She showed it to Betty. "Carrie said Gary came from Pine Valley."

Betty said, "I think I've heard of it. A lot of lumbering operations in that area."

The matches were a clue to where Gary had previously lived, so Shannon set them aside and slid open the top drawer. It held neatly folded boxer shorts and socks, and in one corner, a cache of romantic cards and notes. Shannon selected one, read briefly, and blushed. Now she really felt uncomfortable. But she pulled them out and set them aside to study later. In the second and third drawers, she found only folded T-shirts and jeans and a couple of nice wool sweaters.

"Oops," Betty said, as a piece of folded paper escaped from the book she was shaking. It skittered across the floor and she bent to pick it up. "It's a letter." Scanning the text quickly, she added, "Shannon, you need to read this."

Shannon moved to Betty's side and read over her shoulder.

> *Dear Gary,*
> *I left this in your truck so you would find it. I can't believe you ended things the way you did last night after all your promises to marry me. I thought we had something rare and beautiful. Did I do something wrong? I know things didn't work out with the farm the way we hoped, but relationships are for better or worse, right? I don't blame you, if that's what you're worried about. Please, call me and let's talk.*
> *I love you,*
> *Laura*

"What's going on in here?"

Startled, Shannon and Betty turned to see Hillary in the doorway. Shannon quickly folded the letter and put her hand behind her back.

"I came up to my room to get something, and I saw the door open," Hillary went on, her eyes darting around the room in curiosity.

"Marge asked me to look through Gary's belongings to see if there's anything his relatives might want, if we can

figure out who and where his relatives are." The fewer people who knew she was investigating, the better.

"But he—" Hillary stopped and backed away. "I guess
I'll let you get back to it. Sorry for bothering you." She
poked her head back in. "I think I'll ask for this room once
it's cleaned out. Love the two windows."

"She scared me." Betty put one hand to her chest. "I
almost jumped a mile high."

"Let's shut the door. We don't need anyone else snooping
around." Shannon tucked the letter and the other notes and
cards into her bag. "The letter you found talks about a farm.
I wonder if Gary tried to take over someone else's property
in the past. It seems like we've discovered his M.O."

"And the Laura who wrote that letter could probably
tell us all about it," Betty added.

Finished with the books, Betty moved on to the clothes
hanging in the corner and searched the pockets. Under the
bed, Shannon found a shoebox holding bank statements. "Betty, these are from the bank in town," she said, quickly leafing
through the papers. The first one was dated eighteen months
ago—when Gary had arrived, according to Marge. Shannon
studied the latest one. As in the other months, there were
regular weekly deposits that appeared to be paychecks. She
could verify the amount with Marge. Oddly, there were very
few withdrawals. In the earlier months there had been numer-
ous ones, mostly ATM and local debit-card transactions.

Shannon placed the new statement on the floor beside
an old one.

Betty hunkered down beside her. "What did you find?"

Shannon pointed to the withdrawal columns in both

months. "See the difference? Almost all his pay is spent in that month. Last month, almost none of it."

"What does that mean? He was frugal?"

"You might think that, but the other day, Marge was complaining that the deposits didn't match up. There's a common scam where an employee will skim cash and then replace it later from new cash coming in. I think Gary was doing that."

*   *   *

Back in Apple Grove, Shannon put off doing paperwork and went out to the shed to finish up the pendants instead. She wouldn't have another opportunity to get out there all week, she knew, and customers were waiting to buy them. In a contest between paperwork and customers, customers always won.

Enamel firing times were short, mere minutes, so she was able to apply the multiple layers required for depth of color and texture in a relatively short period of time. While she worked, she purposely didn't think about the case. From past experience, she knew that allowing all the information to percolate in her mind would encourage important clues and conclusions to rise from her subconscious to the forefront. In the background, melodious selections from Bach played on the radio, further setting a mood of peaceful productivity.

Once the firing was done and the jewelry cooled, Shannon soldered on rings to hold the fine silver chains the pendants would hang from.

Who was Gary Booker? The question floated gently into her mind. And once that line of inquiry was raised, other questions followed. Where had he come from, and how had he ended up in Apple Grove? Was it just a coincidence that he had been hired by the Olsons, who desperately needed a second-in-command to take over the farm? Was this indeed his particular scam—taking advantage of vulnerable landowners?

On the surface, the case looked simple. Gary had gotten in Finn's way, and Finn had killed him. But Shannon knew from experience that the truth was often found through careful examination of a person's life. The police, despite their expertise, often gravitated to the most obvious and simple solution. Many of her previous cases attested to this tendency, and it was only Shannon's digging that had revealed the true killer.

The radio announcer reported that it was now four o'clock. Setting down her polishing cloth, Shannon stretched. She'd achieved a good day's output despite the interruption of the trip to the farm. Tonight at home, she'd sit down and figure out what to do next in the investigation. As she padlocked the shed, another serendipitous idea arrived. *Why not ask Jake Stager to help?* With his news background, he was probably an expert at digging into people's backgrounds. Reporters also had access to databases and other sources of information not available to the layperson.

A story for you and a murderer for me, Shannon thought as she pulled out her cellphone and dialed Kate's number, hoping to locate Jake. Walking toward Old Blue, she noticed a piece of paper stuck under the windshield wiper. While waiting for Kate to answer, she casually plucked it off. Another flyer for Apple Grove's Christmas events. They were everywhere. Then she happened to turn it over. What she read sent a chill down her spine.

"STOP OR YOU'RE NEXT" was written in big, simple, block letters.

"Hello, Shannon?" Kate said. "Hello? Are you there?"

"Kate, I just received a death threat."

— 16 —

Shannon hurried down the stairs to answer the mansion's front doorbell. The twins were out with friends, and Deborah had the night off.

She opened the door to find Kate and Jake standing on the porch, Jake holding a big box of pizza. "Perfect timing," Shannon said. "I just got out of the shower." Her tangled red curls were still damp, and she wore a blue fleece top with matching pants and warm, fuzzy slippers. "Please, come in."

The couple stepped into the entryway, dark except for the lights on the magnificent tree decorated with a mix of Victoria's and Shannon's ornaments. Silver tinsel glittered, catching the light from strands of multicolored bulbs. From the very top, a beautiful Italian porcelain angel dressed in silk with real feathered wings watched over them. A lighthouse ornament made by a loft artist and chosen by the twins in honor of their new home in Oregon had its place along with the four angels playing instruments.

Jake whistled. "That's some tree."

"It's gorgeous, Shannon!" Kate exclaimed. "You got that at the farm?"

"Yes. Michael helped me pick it out." Remembering Lara's text of the angel ornaments to Beth, Shannon decided to text a picture of the tree to Michael. "Let's go into the kitchen."

In the kitchen, Shannon gathered stoneware plates from the cupboard along with tall tumblers for soda and iced tea. She'd also thrown together a green salad to go with the pizza, which was topped with a mix of vegetables and pepperoni, and she pulled it from the fridge along with salad dressing selections. Jake opened the box of pizza and Kate put out napkins and shakers of oregano, Parmesan cheese, and red pepper flakes.

For a few minutes, everyone was silent, busily munching on piping-hot pizza and fresh, crunchy salad.

"This is so good," Kate moaned.

"Uh-huh," Shannon agreed. "Anyway, the reason I asked you two over is to see if you want to help me look into Gary Booker's murder."

Jake perked up. "I just filed a story today about Finn Olson's arrest. You think he might not be guilty?"

"There's enough doubt in my mind to check into it further," Shannon replied. She told them about the anonymous email Finn had received. "Plus his mother asked me to."

Jake laughed. "Ah, the mother request. That's a tough one to turn down. Does she understand that you have to tell the police whatever you find, even if it points to Finn?"

Shannon selected a second slice of pizza, sprinkling it liberally with Parmesan cheese. "I already told her that. And then there's that death threat I called Kate about."

"Kate told me about it," Jake said. "You sure seem calm about it."

"It doesn't deter me by any means—in fact, it encourages me. Oh, it gave me a shock at first. Ask Kate. I could barely talk. But usually a threat means I'm on the right track."

Jake raised his eyebrows. "Usually? You go, Shannon."

"I told you," Kate said. "She's good."

"After we eat, I'll show you the threat and the clues I found in Gary Booker's room."

They cleared away the plates and leftovers and Shannon laid out the flyer with the threat, letters, bank statements, and the matchbook she had found. The threat and letter from Laura were in plastic sleeves to preserve fingerprints, although Shannon doubted there would be any. Nothing was ever that simple. Thanks to crime shows, the whole world now knew to wear gloves while carrying out incriminating activities.

Jake examined the flyer carefully, studying both sides of the paper. "There are millions of these floating around town," he said. "And the handwriting isn't distinctive at all."

"That's usually the way," Shannon said. "Unfortunately." She held up the matchbook. "This is the only clue I found to Gary ever being anywhere outside Apple Grove. Strange, isn't it, that he would cover his tracks that way?"

"Let me see that." Kate took the matchbook and scrutinized it, even opening the flap to see if anything was written inside. "Pine Valley. Where have I heard about Pine Valley?" she mused.

"Pine Valley is about a hundred miles south of here," Jake said. "A lot of lumbering and sawmills in that area."

"That's what Betty said," Shannon confirmed. "Makes sense, what with Gary liking to work with trees. He had all kinds of books in his room about tree farming."

"I know," Kate said, her eyes wide. "Hillary came here from Pine Valley. She told me that when I hired her. Her last name is Jenkins, by the way. Hillary Jenkins."

"She has a tree nursery background too," Shannon said. "And now she's living at the farm. It looks like Marge has taken Hillary under her wing."

"Do you think she knew Gary Booker before she moved here?" Kate asked. "She never said anything about him to me."

"I think we need to know more about Gary Booker and Hillary Jenkins from Pine Valley," Jake said. He had the alert air of a bloodhound on the hunt. "Can we use your computer to look them up?"

They went into the study, where Shannon booted up the computer and logged in. Then she let Jake take the chair and do his research magic. She and Kate sat in armchairs nearby and waited.

"Nothing on Gary Booker," Jake said. "Which is really weird. Most people have some kind of online presence these days, even if it's just that they had a phone under their name. Looks like Mr. Booker liked to fly under the radar."

"How about Hillary Jenkins?" Kate asked.

Shannon and Kate watched anxiously while Jake searched, his fingers tapping furiously on the keys. What if they couldn't find anything on her either? They would be at a dead end.

"Aha," Jake finally said. "I've found Hillary Jenkins from Pine Valley."

They scurried over to the computer and peered over Jake's shoulder. "In Memoriam," the top of the page read.

"What does that mean?" Kate gasped.

"It means Hillary Jenkins is dead."

— 17 —

"**D**ead!" Kate exclaimed. "How can that be?"

"Maybe there are two women named Hillary Jenkins," Shannon suggested.

"Hold on, we'll figure this out," Jake said. "Let me read the obit to you."

According to the brief article, Hillary Jenkins had died eight months ago at the age of sixty-five. Her husband, Roger, died the year previous. The only survivors listed were a daughter, Laura, and a sister, Hilda Green; both were residents of Pine Valley.

"Laura. That's the name on the letter we found in Gary's room. Let me get it."

Shannon darted into the kitchen and grabbed the letter. Back in the study, she showed it to the others.

"It sounds like Gary specialized in trying to ingratiate himself with landowners," Jake commented. "I wonder if Roger Jenkins owned any property." He turned back to the computer and began to search.

"What are you looking for?" Kate asked.

"I'm searching the deeds register for that county," Jake replied. "Transfers of ownership, mortgages, and liens are recorded there." After a few minutes, he snorted in disgust. "Nothing under Roger or Hillary Jenkins, now or in the past. But that doesn't mean anything. The land could be held in a corporate name."

"Maybe Laura is using her mother's name," Shannon said. "In any case, something tells me that a Hillary Jenkins showing up here on Gary's heels is not a coincidence."

"Me too," Jake said. "My nose for news is definitely twitching. I think we need to go to Pine Valley since people down there seem to have an aversion to the Internet. The weekly Pine Valley paper is so small they don't even have an online archive. That was the first thing I checked. But I do think we've got enough information to make a trip worthwhile."

"I have a half day tomorrow," Kate said. "Can we go tomorrow afternoon?"

"That will work for me," Shannon said. "I'll ask the twins to help out in the shop. Otherwise I'll be in deep trouble with Essie. I've been leaving her to handle things too often lately."

*   *   *

The next morning at the shop, Shannon was dispensing coffees and hot chocolates when Chaz came in. "Thanks again for letting us put trees out there," he said. "We've sold tons."

"No problem, Chaz. I'm glad it's working out for you," she said. "What can I get you?"

"Two large coffees. To go."

Carrie came into the coffee shop. "Do you need me in here or should I work in the craft shop today?" Although she still looked tired, Carrie was almost her old spunky self again, Shannon was glad to see.

Dispensing coffee into paper cups, Shannon said, "The twins will be down soon, and they can work in here. How about pricing the sale items in the yarn area? Essie knows which ones we're reducing."

"Sure thing."

As Carrie started to walk away, Chaz blurted, "Aren't you Gary Booker's girlfriend?"

Carrie stopped dead, her cheeks reddening. "Um, not really."

Chaz snapped his fingers and pointed at her. "I saw you at the farm the day Gary … you know."

"No, you couldn't have."

Shannon paused in putting the caps on the coffee, her curiosity aroused. According to Carrie, she hadn't seen Gary since the ill-fated dinner at the inn.

"Yes, it *was* you. I recognize that." He waved his hand around his head, indicating her dark, curly hair. "I got up to use the bathroom, and I saw you coming out of his room."

"Why don't you mind your own business?" she snapped, stalking into the other room.

Chaz laughed ruefully. "My mouth always gets me into trouble." He paid Shannon with several worn dollar bills and carried the two coffees away, whistling.

After the twins arrived, Shannon decided to tackle her sadly neglected paperwork. But first there was someone she needed to talk to. Passing the yarn area, she told Carrie, "Please come with me." She heard an exasperated sigh and a clunk as Carrie put down the pricing gun, but she ignored both.

Inside the office, Carrie flung herself into a chair and stared at Shannon defiantly.

Shannon knew her attitude was ninety-nine percent embarrassment at being caught in a lie, so she didn't react.

"Carrie," she said evenly. "Why don't you tell me about your visit to Gary? I don't think I heard anything about that."

Carrie stared at her lap, picking at a piece of lint on her black corduroy pants. "I was too humiliated to talk about it."

Shannon lowered her voice, speaking gently. "The last thing I want to do is embarrass you or pry into your personal life. But everything that happened that day concerning Gary and the farm is important. You may have seen something that will lead to his killer."

Carrie's head jerked up. "You mean Finn might not be guilty?"

Shannon shrugged. "It's too soon to say. Marge asked me to help investigate, so I am. That's all."

"All right. I'll tell you." Carrie crossed her arms in front of her chest. "I went over there early in the morning to talk to him. Real early, before anyone was out of bed. I regretted our fight, and I thought maybe we could patch things up." She grimaced. "But he turned me down."

Ouch. "Did he say why?" Shannon asked. "You're a pretty girl, Carrie," she added, to soothe the poor thing's ego. "He was lucky you were interested in him."

Carrie laughed, a bitter and wretched little bark. "Thanks for saying that. For once I don't think it had anything to do with another woman. Or women. He said, 'I have bigger problems to deal with right now.' That's a quote."

"Do you know what those problems were?" Shannon could guess. Finn had been on his case, and Gary must have been concerned that his position at the farm was tenuous.

"I have no idea. I just know that I've never been so mortified in my life."

Mortified enough to kill Gary? Shannon hated to suspect her employee, but she knew that she had to keep an open mind. Almost anyone could kill under the right circumstances. And who had left that threat on her windshield?

She needed to talk to Finn. Once again, the paperwork could wait.

*   *   *

Officer Brownley escorted Shannon to Finn's cell. Apple Grove's jail had only two singles, and if Finn wasn't released on bail, he'd be headed to the county jail until trial.

"I'll give you ten minutes," Brownley said, unlocking the cell and allowing Shannon to enter. He slammed it shut with a clang, and the sound made chills run down her spine. *How horrible to be locked in, away from everything and everyone you love.*

Finn sat slumped on the narrow bunk, his head lowered in depression. When he glanced up, his eyes were bleak, shadowed by dark circles. He hadn't shaved for a couple of days, and the scruff plus his unwashed locks made him look like someone sliding into a trough of despair. "Did my mother send you?'

Shannon glanced at the open door to the main part of the station where Brownley sat, probably listening. She lowered her voice. "Kind of. I promised I'd investigate Gary's death. When is your arraignment?"

"This afternoon. I might not get bail. They think I'm a flight risk because I've been living overseas. Of course, they already confiscated my passport, but apparently they believe

I might have connections to get out of the country anyway. What a joke. I'm a teacher, not a terrorist." He hit his knee with his fist. "Why did I ever come back here? I was happy in Singapore."

"Let's talk about why you came back, Finn. Your mother told me about an email you received. Any idea who sent it?"

He shook his head vehemently. "None. I wouldn't have even paid attention to it except it linked to the Apple Grove planning board's website. That's where I saw exactly what Gary Booker was cooking up." His tone was bitter. "Yeah, I admit I hated that guy. Who wouldn't? He had Mom and Dad enamored to the point they were going to make me share my inheritance with him."

Shannon sympathized, but she made the point anyway. "Gary did a lot to help your parents run the farm, according to them."

"I'm sure that's true. And I don't have a problem with someone getting what they deserve for the effort they put in. But when I found out he convinced them to subdivide, I just knew something was wrong." He jabbed a thumb toward his chest. "I actually suggested it years ago, when they were struggling. Dad bit my head off for even daring to bring it up. Now Gary does, and it's so great they're going to make him part owner? I don't think so."

His voice had risen and Shannon put a hand on his knee, shushing him. If he kept losing his temper, they'd convict him for sure. "Finn, keep it down. Gary can't hurt you or your parents anymore. But if we want to get you out of here, we need to find out who killed him." Once he'd settled down, she went on. "I got an anonymous note too."

"What do you mean?"

"Someone left a threatening note under the wiper of my truck yesterday. It told me to back off from looking into the murder. In so many words."

Finn's face lit up. "That's proof I didn't do it!"

"It might well be. Tell me about your visit to see Carrie Saturday morning."

An odd look crossed his face. "You don't suspect her, do you?"

"Right now I'm just gathering information. Someone told me that on Saturday morning, she visited Gary at the farm."

"I know. I saw her leaving, sneaking across the farmyard to her car. I couldn't believe that my old girlfriend was dating that snake."

Shannon thought of something. "Your mother said you left the farm midweek. But you went back?"

Finn's expression was sheepish. "Yeah. After the second fight with Gary, I decided to stay at a motel. I have proof if you want it. Receipts. But I had to go get my bow and arrows for the hunting trip to Misner's. I'd left them in the barn."

"Tell me, were all your arrows there?"

"Yep. I had a dozen. We count 'em, you know. They cost too much to just let them fly off and leave them behind. I always retrieve them after I shoot."

"While you were visiting Carrie, did you leave your equipment in the car?"

"Of course. In the trunk. I was still using a rental car then."

"And Carrie never went outside her apartment without you?"

He shook his head. "I wasn't there that long."

So Finn had had all his arrows that day, and Carrie hadn't had an opportunity to remove any from his bag. Sometime between Saturday morning and the arrest on Monday, someone had stolen two of his arrows. To frame him? According to his statement, Finn hadn't come back to the farm until after Gary's body was discovered.

"What did you and Carrie talk about?"

For the first time, a smile cracked Finn's somber façade. "After we stopped shouting, you mean? I couldn't believe that she had fallen for that piece of work, and I told her so. In return, she chewed me out for abandoning my parents. And her. You see, back in high school, we'd talked about getting married. Then I went off to college, and we broke up." He shrugged. "I didn't realize she still cared that much."

"So then what?"

A red tide crept up Finn's neck, turning his ears bright crimson. "Ah, well. We, um ..."

"Renewed your relationship?" Shannon suggested.

Again, his shoulders jerked in a shrug. "Sort of. Not much happened. Just a couple of kisses."

Shannon felt like she was hearing the confession of a hapless teenager. "None of my business," she said briskly. "Thanks for answering my questions." She moved toward the cell door, ready to call to Brownley to let her out.

"What's next?" he asked.

"Later today, I'm taking a road trip."

"You think you can get me off? I'd love an opportunity to mend the fence with my folks. Maybe even try with Carrie again."

"I'll do my best." She studied him for a moment, noticing a flicker of hope in his eyes. "In the meantime, keep your chin up. I'll be in touch. Maybe you'll get the opportunity you're looking for to make things right."

Walking back to the market from the jail, Shannon decided to pop into Pink Sprinkles Bakery for treats to take along on the ride to Pine Valley. Big signs in the window advertised Joyce's Twelve Days of Christmas Cookies promotion.

Inside, Bill Buchanan watched as Joyce packed up a large box of cookies, muffins, and pastries.

"Good morning, Shannon!" Joyce called. "What can I do for you?"

"Are you having a staff meeting too?" Bill asked. "I always find they go better when I bring treats." He smiled at his wife. "They think I'm a great manager, but it's really because of Joyce that my employees are so happy."

Joyce laughed. "Maybe I'll give you a discount for saying that." She tied a polka-dot ribbon around the box and made a big bow.

Shannon studied the double-decker cookie case. Long trays of cookies were placed side by side, hand-written placards announcing the cookie name and country. "I'm going out of town today, and I wanted to bring some snacks along. Gosh, I don't know whether to choose cookies from Jamaica, Greece, or Austria."

Bill joined Shannon in front of the case, holding his box in both hands. "I was pretty amazed that Joyce found all those new recipes."

"How about picking ones you've never tried?" Joyce suggested.

"Good idea. I'd like three each of the Venetian bar cookies, the German lebkuchen, and the Jamaican coconut pralines, please."

"Great choice." Joyce selected cookies and placed them gently into a box lined with tissue paper.

"I've been working with Marge Olson on some bookkeeping discrepancies in her accounts," Bill said to Shannon. At her look of surprise, he added, "She gave me permission to talk about it to you."

"She said something about that the other day, and honestly, I thought it was fishy then," Shannon said. "It sounded like someone had been holding back cash and then making up the difference later from new money coming in. So someone was stealing?"

Bill's lip quirked in a crooked smile. "They'd probably say 'borrowing,' but yes, several hundred dollars are unaccounted for."

"Gary's death brought the little scam to a screeching halt, I guess."

"Since he made the deposits, I'd say yes," Bill said. "On another topic, are you joining us at the ice rink tonight?"

"Over at the park?"

"Yes. The ice is finally ready. The whole community usually comes out. It's fun."

"I haven't skated in years," Shannon said. "I'll probably look like a fool."

"If you don't have skates, they rent them," Bill added helpfully.

"Bill and I ice-dance together," Joyce said. She twirled and swooped in demonstration.

"*That* I've got to see," Shannon said with a laugh.

Bill winked. "We're not bad. Won a contest or two back in the day. Well, this is fun, ladies, but I'd better get to the bank. The meeting starts in five minutes. See you later."

"Bye, dear. See you at home. I'll dig out the skates."
Joyce packed up Shannon's cookies. "Here you go. Enjoy."
Her smile was a trifle wicked. "And I want to hear all about
your trip at the next Purls meeting. You're off to investigate
Gary Booker's death, right?"

"How did you know?"

"Betty told me. Good luck. It'd be nice for the Olsons if
it was all wrapped up before Christmas."

"I'll do my best."

The bells over the door jangled and several middle-
aged women carrying shopping bags bustled in, poring over
the bakery's array of tasty, tempting treats and enjoying
the tempting smells. Smiling, Shannon threaded her way
through them toward the door. Nothing like sugar to give
you energy to shop. Or play detective.

Carrying the box of cookies, Shannon continued on
her way to the craft market. She also hoped the investigation would wrap up soon so she could concentrate on her
customers. Essie and Carrie were being stretched almost
beyond their limits during the busy Christmas season. She
would hate for them to quit on her right now. Good thing
the twins were around to help. They enjoyed making some
extra money too.

As she approached the market, Chaz waved at her from
his post in the Christmas tree lot at the end of the building.
"How's it going, Mrs. McClain?" he called.

Shannon detoured to say hello. A short distance away,
she saw Hillary helping a family load a tree onto a Jeep's
roof. "Everything going well?" Shannon asked.

"Awesome. We get lots of customers here." Grinning,

he nodded at the busy street where constant streams of cars passed in both directions. "It's gonna be another good day. I can tell."

"That's great. Well, I've got to go. See you later, Chaz." As Shannon turned away, she noticed Hillary's backpack sitting beside the canvas folding chairs she and Chaz used between customers. A patch in the middle of the colorful collection caught her eye: round, with yellow, red, and blue circles. Carrie had a ribbon like that too. She'd have to ask her what it meant.

Despite having just opened for the day, the craft market was humming with activity already. Essie was showing a handsome, well-dressed man one of Shannon's completed pendants, while Carrie rang up a big stack of merchandise for a woman Shannon recognized as a regular. The twins were furiously fielding requests for hot drinks and pastries in the coffee shop. Shannon pitched in to help, and before she knew it, it was almost time to meet Kate and Jake at Ultimutt Grooming. Her last task was calling in a lunch order to a local restaurant. She'd pick up sandwiches for the trip on the walk to Kate's shop. The restaurant would deliver the rest to the store for her crew. Bill's advice had resonated: Feed them well to keep them happy!

Loaded down with the pastry box and a big paper bag, Shannon met Jake at the door of Ultimutt. "Good timing," he said as he held the door open for her. Inside, Kate was behind the counter. Today her shirt depicted a cat looking insulted with text reading "What do you mean, YOU own ME?" Through the open door to the grooming room, her new helper, a dark-haired young woman, could be seen trimming a huge Newfoundland with a clipper.

Kate laughed when she saw the pink box. Reaching under the counter, she pulled out an identical one. "Great minds think alike," she said. "What did you get? I got the Canadian custard-filled, the apricot Linzer cookies, and the Greek honey balls."

Shannon told them her selections and added, "We'll certainly be well fueled for the ride."

"I guess," Jake said. "I put a cooler with water and soda in the SUV, so we're all set for drinks. Are we ready to roll?"

"Almost," Kate said. "I have to tell Miranda something." She stuck her head into the other room and spoke to her assistant.

A moment later, Miranda entered the main shop with Boyd on a leash. When he spotted Shannon, he lurched forward, his nails scrabbling on the slippery floor, and Miranda had to strain to hold him back. "Good thing I'm strong," Miranda said with a laugh. "He sure wants to go to you."

Her remark reminded Shannon of Hillary, who seemed to handle big, awkward trees with ease, despite her bumbling appearance. Could she actually be Laura Jenkins, incognito here in Apple Grove for her own reasons? Shannon hoped they would learn the answer today. Finn's freedom depended on the success of their trip to Pine Valley.

Kate introduced everyone and then added with a sly smile, "I thought we'd bring Boyd along. He needs to get out once in a while. I'll carry the food. Here." She took the leash from Miranda and handed it to Shannon. Boyd immediately began to lick Shannon's leather boots and the knee of her jeans. She patted his fuzzy head, surprisingly glad to see him again. There was something ridiculously flattering about having an animal adore you, she decided, not to mention the fact that she could feel some of her stress melting away just from the dog's happy-go-lucky attitude. Maybe she could keep some of that calm once they got to Pine Valley.

— 18 —

For the drive to Pine Valley, Jake chose U.S. Route 101, which wound along the rugged coastline. Around each corner were stunning vistas of rocky cliffs tumbling down to crystalline waters that rushed and roared, breaking against huge boulders. In some spots, the road skirted lonely beaches inhabited only by seagulls. Shannon sat in the back, allowing the lovebirds to sit up front together. Boyd rode in the cargo area, strapped in securely. But he could still reach Shannon's hair with his nose, and once in a while, he nuzzled her, reminding her that he was there.

Watching Kate and Jake laughing and chatting up front made Shannon smile. She could barely hear what they were saying, but their body language spoke volumes. The growing connection between them was revealed by frequent glances, touches on the arm as one or the other made a point, the whispers and shared jokes. Shannon was happy for her friend. She'd been single a long time, often despairing of finding someone truly compatible.

Shannon took out her phone, wishing Michael would call or text. His flight to Japan took twelve hours and their time zone was sixteen hours ahead ... it might be another day before he would have a chance to call. Tonight was the earliest, probably. Although the last two days had flown by, the awareness that he was far away, on the other side of the world, hovered in the back of her mind. She missed him!

As if sensing her sadness, Boyd nuzzled her hair and whimpered. "You're a good boy," she told him.

They stopped briefly at an overlook to eat turkey sandwiches and cookies and let Boyd out to walk around. They were the only ones there, and as they sat on big boulders, looking out at the sparkling, dancing Pacific Ocean, Shannon again thought of Michael. He was on the other side of the world, across that big expanse of blue water.

*   *   *

Waking up in his room at Tokyo's Hotel Okura, Michael's first thought was of Shannon. He glanced at the bright red digits on the alarm clock. Five a.m. That meant it was noon in Apple Grove. He pictured what she was probably doing right now: bustling around the store, waiting on customers, blessing them with her friendly smiles and kind words. *Ah, Shannon* ... she was truly lovely.

Outside the window, he heard the first sounds of a large city waking up. The Hotel Okura was considered a luxury hotel, and it spoke well of Michael's client that he was putting up Michael's team here. The amenities were tailored to American executives, yet the place oozed with Japanese charm and style. Besides eight restaurants and four lounges, the hotel had indoor and outdoor pools and a full workout center. The train station was mere blocks away, convenient for getting around the city.

Throwing back the duvet, he stood up, stretching, debating whether to call Shannon. He wanted to hear her voice, which still retained soft traces of a Scottish burr. He'd read online that Finn Olson had been arrested, and he wondered what Shannon thought of that.

I hope she doesn't get herself in trouble.

He drew back the drapes and looked out at the view of Tokyo. With Shannon's customers and employees listening in, it wasn't a good time to call, he decided. He'd call tonight, after the market closed. That meant staying up until midnight after a full day on-site with the client. He'd just have to drink plenty of coffee to stay awake.

* * *

Soon Jake left 101 and took the road inland to Pine Valley. Although about the same size as Apple Grove in population, Pine Valley's outskirts, architecture, and businesses reflected its history as a wood industry town. Half-empty wood yards and lumber mills surrounded a downtown that had seen better days. The brick blocks lining Main Street were shabby, many of the storefronts vacant. Only a few pedestrians were about, a big contrast to Apple Grove's bustling sidewalks. They passed the Miss Oregon Diner, located in an old train car; a bank with a stopped clock; a hardware store; two gas stations on opposite corners; and assorted small retail shops.

"This town, along with many others around here, was hit hard with the recession," Jake said. "The slump in housing decimated Oregon's wood industry." Jake pulled to a stop in front of a one-story yellow-brick building with tall plate-glass windows. The faded sign over the door read "Pine Valley News."

"OK, what's our cover story?" Kate asked with a giggle. "I've been on a stakeout myself. I know a little about detective work."

"I'm going to say I'm covering the wood industry," Jake said. "These small towns can be pretty insular, and if I go in there asking a bunch of questions about Gary Booker, they might clam up. However, if they offer information, I'll let them run with it, of course."

"And we'll try to find Laura's aunt," Shannon said. "And then play it by ear."

"Being a detective and a reporter have a lot in common," Jake commented. "Reading people for cues is key."

Leaving Boyd in the SUV with the windows down far enough for plenty of air, the trio went inside the newspaper office. As they entered the small vestibule, the first thing that struck Shannon was the strong and slightly unpleasant smell of ink. Jake noticed it too. "They must still be printing here. Most papers outsource that now."

An elderly woman with curly gray hair and cat-eye glasses sat at a desk behind a waist-high counter in the main room. She wore a blue cardigan around her shoulders, held in place with a chain, and polyester pants and top in the same color. A gold nameplate on the counter read "Esther Shaw." The two other desks in the room were empty, and stacks of newspapers sat in a wire basket near the door. "Former Local Man Dead," screamed the headlines. *Gary's death must be the biggest news in Pine Valley*, Shannon thought.

With a hand to her back, Esther stood up. "Good afternoon. You here to place an ad?" A broad smile revealing big white dentures confirmed she was happy to have her isolation interrupted.

Jake took the lead. "Actually, I'd like to look at your

archives. I'm researching a story on the rebound in the wood industry." He slid his press pass across the counter.

Esther peered at the pass, her mouth turned down in a doubtful frown. "If it was rebounding around here, that'd be good. But we haven't seen much sign of it yet." Her gesture encompassed the dreary streets outside her window.

"I'm sorry to hear that," Jake said. "Overall indicators are good, though."

"All we have in the archive are paper issues bound into books," she warned. "Nothing is on computer."

Jake laughed. "I know. That's why we drove down here from Apple Grove."

Esther brightened even more. "Apple Grove? That's where Gary Booker met his demise." She picked up a newspaper from her desktop and waved it. "Just came out in today's issue. Biggest news around here since the lumber mill downsized." She leaned across the counter eagerly, her eyes gleaming behind the glasses. "Do you have any inside information on the case? The latest we have is an Apple Grove man was arrested. Do you know him?"

Shannon and Kate looked to Jake for guidance. He shook his head ruefully. "Not my beat, I'm afraid. You were a reporter, weren't you, Mrs. Shaw? I can always tell."

She cackled. "Call me Esther. Sure was. Still fill in once in a while when our reporter can't get to a meeting or something." She waved the paper again. "We might be just a weekly, but the upside is we cover things in depth."

"I respect that," Jake said. "I started on a weekly myself."

"Well, I suppose I shouldn't stand here yammering," Esther said. "Let me show you the archives." She opened a gate in the counter. "All three of you going back?"

"No," Shannon said. "We just came along for the ride, and while we're here, we want to look up Hilda Green. We know her niece, Laura."

"I can help you with that. Just let me get this young fella settled." She hustled Jake through a door at the back of the room. Shannon caught a glimpse of a hallway leading to the rear of the building. Within minutes, Esther was back, her expression alight with inquiry. "So how do you know Laura Jenkins?" She leaned on the counter, obviously ready for an extended chat.

"Um, she works for me," Kate said. "I own a pet grooming service in Apple Grove."

"Really? That's a switch. Laura used to work on her family's tree farm. Pine Valley Tree Farm." She cackled again. "Not too creative a name, huh?"

"You said 'used to.' Is the tree farm still operating?" Shannon asked.

Esther shook her head sadly. "Nope. Went downhill after Roger Jenkins died. And then the bank foreclosed after Hillary, Laura's mother, passed away. Overextended, like so many others around here. Another sad Pine Valley story." Her gaze grew suspicious. "Laura didn't tell you all this?"

"Oh, she alluded to it," Kate assured Esther. "But I think she's still in mourning, so I didn't want to pry."

Esther gave a sharp nod. "Understandable. Not only did she lose her parents, but her livelihood too. That's a lot for anyone to handle. Leaving town was probably a good move." She tapped one finger on her lips, thinking. "How's she handling Gary's death? Poor thing, another blow. He worked at the tree farm, you know."

Shannon and Kate exchanged looks. Here it was, proof that Laura Jenkins knew Gary Booker. Now they just needed proof that Hillary was actually Laura.

"She's OK," Shannon said hurriedly. All they needed was for Esther to really think about the coincidence that both Laura and Gary had ended up in the same small town. "Where can we find her aunt?" She glanced at the wall clock to give the impression that they didn't have much time.

"Hilda Green? You'll find her at the diner, probably. She's the owner." Esther pointed out the window to the left. "Just down the street a block or two. Close enough to walk, if you want."

"We'll do that. Thanks. You've been very helpful." As they left the newspaper office, Shannon could feel Esther's eyes on them.

"That woman is entirely too sharp," Kate murmured once they reached the safety of the outdoors.

"She sure is. I hope Jake can withstand her questioning."

Boyd gave a little yip as they approached the SUV. "Let's take him with us," Shannon suggested. "Poor guy has been cooped up almost all day."

They let Boyd out, rolled up the windows, and locked the car. Then they set off down the sidewalk toward the diner. Shannon walked Boyd, who trotted along, happy to sniff the fire hydrants and mailboxes in a new town. They passed a storefront block hosting a barbershop, secondhand bookstore, and a consignment shop.

"Our main issue is connecting Hillary to Laura, right?" Kate asked.

"That's the first thing we need to do, yes. But we also

need to know if she was capable of shooting him with a bow and arrow." Shannon stopped dead. "I just thought of something. I've got to call Carrie."

Kate took the leash while Shannon dug out her cellphone and called the store. Inside the barbershop, several old men peered out, curious to see newcomers in town. Kate waved at them.

"Hi, Essie. It's Shannon. How's it going?"

"Fantastic," Essie replied, sounding harried. "Busy. I sold three of your pendants. Thanks for the lunch, by the way."

"No problem. Can you put Carrie on, please?"

"Sure thing." Shannon heard the receiver being set down with a clunk on the counter and Essie's voice calling Carrie.

"Hello?" Carrie, too, sounded breathless.

"Hi, Carrie. I won't keep you long. Remember your trophies and ribbons? Which sport does the round colored one go to?"

"Archery. You get it if you hit the bull's-eye in a competition. I got mine at the state meet in high school. Why?"

"Oh, I saw one somewhere," Shannon said, then wished she could take it back.

Too late. Carrie made the leap. "Oh, someone who might have killed Gary, you mean. Who was it?"

"Don't ask." At Shannon's distressed tone, Boyd whined, nudging her leg with his nose. "It's a dangerous situation. It's best if you forget I said anything."

Carrie snorted. "OK. I'll mind my own business." She switched her tone to a more conciliatory one. "We're doing great today. The twins have been awesome. Just thought you might want to know that, boss. See you when you get back."

"What's up, Shannon?" Kate asked as they began walking again.

"Today I took another look at Hillary's backpack. Not on purpose; it was just sitting there outside, next to her chair. According to Carrie, one of her patches is for high school archery."

Kate sucked in a surprised breath. "Oh, that could be evidence."

"She'd probably say she bought it as part of her collection. We need to find proof that she knows how to shoot."

"I have an idea." Kate pointed at a pretty little brick building across the street, set back in the middle of a big lawn. It had stained glass windows and copper trim on its multi-gabled roof. "Let's try the library. They often have high school yearbooks. If Hillary—or, should I say, Laura— was on the team, we'll find out in those."

Katie tied Boyd to the bike rack and they went into the library, which fortunately was open. Most small-town libraries had limited hours, as Shannon had found when returning books in Apple Grove. Instead of getting a new book, she'd had to settle for a vintage Lord Peter Wimsey mystery novel she'd found in the mansion library. Then she'd gone back to the library for the rest of the series.

The young woman checking in books at the front desk looked up with a smile. This time of day, there weren't many patrons in the little library, which consisted of two side rooms and a back room all off a circular central lobby. Sunlight danced through the stained glass transom windows, and the air had that indescribable library odor of old books, dust, and wood that Shannon loved.

"Can I help you?" the young woman asked. Her nameplate read "Connie Shelton, Head Librarian," and she appeared to be in her mid-thirties, blond, and attractive in a round-faced, pleasingly plump way.

Shannon let Kate take the lead. "I was wondering if you have old Pine Valley high school yearbooks here," she said.

"Are you looking for Gary Booker? He didn't go to school here."

Kate put on a puzzled expression. "Who's Gary Booker?"

The woman sighed. "Some guy who used to live here and got murdered up north somewhere. The press has been digging around for background info."

"They can be pretty pushy," Shannon agreed, smiling innocently. She winked at Kate. "We're not the press, I assure you. So where are the yearbooks?"

Without further questions, the woman pointed to the reference room. "In there, in the Local History section." Unlike Esther, Connie apparently didn't have an ounce of curiosity. Great for them, not so good for befuddled researchers using the library, Shannon suspected.

An elderly man reading a newspaper at one of the tables didn't even look up as they entered and scanned the bookcases for the history section. The yearbooks, all the same size but different colors, marched along the bottom shelf in the corner. Shannon and Kate kneeled down in front of the books. "What year?" Shannon whispered. She slid one out that read *1950 Woodchucks*. Woodchucks must have been the high school mascot.

"She told me she's twenty-eight, so I'd say ten years ago. Let's get some from either side of that date too."

Loaded with books, they sat at the other empty table and began to flip through the pages, seeking out the senior section. "It's funny," Kate commented, earning a glare and a harsh rattle of pages from the newspaper reader. She lowered her voice. "This yearbook could be from any school anywhere." She pointed at senior portraits. "The homecoming queen." Blond and gorgeous. "The football player." Handsome and square-jawed. "The nerd." A geek with big black glasses.

"We don't have these in Scotland," Shannon whispered. "What were you?"

With another ostentatious rattle of the newspaper as he folded it up, the elderly man got up and toddled from the room, jamming on his hat as he went. Good. They could relax now and not worry about bothering anyone.

Kate pointed to a pretty, athletic-looking girl. "I was a jock." She quickly leafed ahead to the J's. "Ta-da. Laura Jenkins."

Laura Jenkins wore her dark hair parted in the middle and pulled back. Although not beautiful, she was good-looking in a straightforward way, her gaze direct over unsmiling lips.

"Is that her, do you think?" Shannon asked, tracing her finger over Laura's printed face.

Kate peered at the photo closely, squinting her eyes. "I think so. Add the curly hair—it's dyed by the way; I noticed her roots one day when she was bending down—and glasses, and it's her, all right. See, she's got a little dimple in her chin."

Shannon stared at the picture, trying to picture Laura as Hillary. "She did a good job disguising herself."

"Part of it is body language. Hillary tends to keep her head down and walk like she's uncoordinated. She also wears clothes that are too baggy. I thought at first it was because she had lost a lot of weight and couldn't afford new ones." Kate grinned. "I know all about that. But maybe she was never overweight to begin with. It was part of her camouflage."

"She acted like she was weak and out of shape too," Shannon said. "Then today I saw her lifting a big tree like it was a feather."

Kate pulled out her cellphone and snapped a picture of Laura's senior portrait. "Now let's see if she was on the archery team."

Laura appeared to have been quite athletic. She was a star member of the field hockey and basketball teams, evidenced by candid shots as well as team photos. Archery didn't seem to be a prominent sport at the school since there was only one small picture included near the end of the sports section. Below a row of a dozen girls smiling and clutching bows, the name "L. Jenkins" was listed.

"Ah, there we go," Kate said with satisfaction. She took a photograph of the team, careful to make sure the names were in focus, even if the faces were almost indistinguishable in the photo.

Shannon sat quietly for a minute to let all they'd learned sink in. It certainly looked like Hillary Jenkins was actually Laura. And, even more crucial, she knew how to handle a bow and arrow well enough to compete. Circumstantial evidence perhaps, but she hoped it was enough to shed doubt on Finn's guilt.

*   *   *

Finn stood in front of the judge, his hands clammy with anxiety. His parents sat on the benches behind him, and without looking, he could sense their mingled hope and fear.

"You can see the defendant is a flight risk," the prosecutor said. "He's lived out of the country for years. He lacks strong ties to Apple Grove, and with the heinous nature of the crime, I recommend that bail be denied." He sat down, a smug look on his face.

Now Finn's lawyer stood. "Your Honor, I respectfully disagree. Finn Olson returned to Apple Grove because of his deep concern regarding his parents. He has pled not guilty to the crime, and I think it will be to everyone's benefit if he can stay with his parents until trial. They need his assistance in running the farm. I ask that bail be granted, with the condition that he not leave the area."

Judge Katherine Anderson, an older woman with sleek dark hair and striking good looks, studied Finn. He did his best to stand up straight, knowing that he looked wretched despite his efforts to clean up for the hearing. Nerves no doubt stretched to the breaking point, his mother gave a brokenhearted whimper, followed by a gentle shushing from his father.

Perhaps his mother's reaction influenced the judge's ruling. "Bail is set at two hundred fifty thousand dollars," she said firmly. "Defendant is to remain in the county until trial." She banged her gavel. "You are free to go."

Marge burst into tears. The prosecutor groaned under his breath. Finn's heart sang with jubilation. He knew he was required to provide only ten percent of the bail amount, and he had that in savings. He took a deep, cleansing breath, the first since being arrested. Thanks to a kindhearted judge, he was free. And he had every intention of staying that way—permanently.

— 19 —

Shannon and Kate left the library to find Boyd enjoying being the center of attention of a group of children. "Is this your dog?" a little blond girl wearing a pink backpack asked. The bike rack was filling up now as youngsters arrived at the library, obviously a favorite after-school destination.

"Yes, he is," Kate said. "Go ahead, you can pet him. He's friendly."

The girl reached out a tentative hand and touched his head. "Oh! He's fuzzy," she said, surprised. Boyd licked her fingers, which sent her into a charming fit of giggles.

"What's his name?" a boy asked, his freckled face solemn under a navy blue wool cap. He darted forward and stroked the dog's back.

"Boyd," Shannon said. "It means 'yellow' in Gaelic."

"What's 'Gaelic'?" a dark-haired girl wanted to know.

"It's a language I used to speak in Scotland," Shannon explained. "*Dè an t-ainm a tha oirbh?* That means, 'What's your name?'"

"Rebecca," the girl with the pink backpack squealed in delight.

"*Is mise* Shannon," she said. "My name is Shannon."

"*Is mise* Joe," the freckled boy said. He pointed at Boyd. "*Is mise* Boyd."

"Hello, Rebecca, Joe," Kate said. "*Is mise* Kate."

After everyone had a turn at saying "*Is mise*," Shannon

and Kate were finally able to pull Boyd away from his admiring audience and head down the street to the diner.

"How should we handle talking to Laura's aunt?" Kate asked.

"We don't know if they're still in touch," Shannon said. "So let's act like we don't suspect anything. We just happened to be here in town, and Laura asked us to stop by and say hello."

"I'll follow your lead," Kate decided. "You've got a lot more experience than me in being a detective. I'd hate to blurt out the wrong thing and mess everything up."

"The last thing we want to do is tip Laura off," Shannon said. "Desperate people do desperate things."

*   *   *

"Hey, guys," Carrie said, holding out two tall paper cups to Chaz and Hillary, who were sitting in their folding chairs, waiting for customers. "I thought you might like some hot chocolate."

"All *right*," Chaz said, eagerly reaching for one of the cups. "How'd you know I was thinking about coming in for one?"

Carrie laughed. "I figured as much. It's getting cold out. See?" She exhaled her breath, demonstrating the plume of vapor it made.

"Good. The ice rink will hold up," Chaz said. "We're going over tonight. How about you?"

Carrie shrugged. "Maybe. After the store closes."

"You should. They have music and food and stuff. It's fun."

A woman wandered up and began looking at a display of wreaths decorated with berries and bows and ornaments. Hillary put her cocoa in the chair's cupholder and said, "I'll get this."

Carrie plopped down into her vacated chair. Her gaze fell

on Hillary's pack, ornamented with patches and buttons. "Is that hers?"

Chaz nodded. "Yep. It's pretty cool, isn't it? Like those wreaths she made. Most people have their trees by now, so Hillary started putting together wreaths back at the farm. Sold about twenty of 'em today."

The woman bought the wreath, carrying it away proudly, and Hillary came toward them clutching a twenty and a five-dollar bill. "Open the cash box for me," she instructed Chaz. She placed the money carefully in the right slots, then fixed her gaze on Carrie. "You're in my seat."

Carrie jumped up with a laugh. "I know. Sorry. I'd better get back inside." She paused, pointing at the pack. "See that circular patch? The bull's-eye? I have one just like it." She gave Hillary a sly grin. "I won it at an archery competition."

"Archery? Cool," Chaz muttered in the background. Neither woman heard him; instead, they continued to stare at each other intently, like two cats preparing to fight.

"Why don't you come skating tonight?" Hillary said. "I'd like to talk to you about archery."

Carrie tossed her head and smiled smugly. "I just might. See you then ... Hillary. Chaz."

* * *

In Pine Valley, the afternoon had warmed up enough to make being outside a delight rather than unpleasant, so Shannon and Kate decided to sit in a sheltered corner of the diner's deck, which was empty in the lull between lunch and dinner. Since they were outside, Boyd was allowed to remain with them, curled up under the table in the shade. While they waited for a server to come out, they looked over the laminated menus left on the table. They displayed the typical diner fare of comfort foods like meat loaf and macaroni and cheese as well as traditional American sandwiches and burgers.

"What should we have?" Kate mused. "I'm not the least bit hungry after that lunch and all those cookies."

"It says they're famous for their pie. We should order some so we can get on Hilda's good side."

"How about splitting a piece of the chocolate cream? Or you can order it and I'll have a bite. I've been doing so well with my exercise regimen that I can eat some sweets. But I still need to be careful." Kate had long struggled with her weight and had recently dropped over twenty pounds.

"That sounds good. I'd like coffee and water too."

The waitress, a thin teenager with long, dishwater-blond hair pulled into a ponytail, bustled out the door carrying two glasses of ice water. "Sorry to keep you waiting." Boyd stuck his nose out from under the table and touched her stocking-clad leg, making her jump. "Who's this? What a nice dog! Want me to bring him a water dish?"

"That'd be great, thanks." Shannon ordered the pie and coffee, then asked, "Is Hilda in?"

The waitress rolled her eyes. "Of course. She lives here practically." Her tone was fond if exasperated.

"If she has time, we'd love to talk to her," Kate said. "Her niece works for me up in Apple Grove, and she wanted us to stop by and say hi."

The waitress's mouth dropped open. "Laura? I wondered where she went. Everyone did. I know Hilda will want to hear this. Be right back with your order."

She was true to her word, flying back onto the deck in less than five minutes carrying a tray with two mugs of coffee, cream, sugar, and a mountainous piece of chocolate cream pie. "It's to die for," she said, placing the pie in the middle of the table along with two forks. "Real whipped cream. I'll bring the dog his water in a sec. Hilda said she'd be right out."

Shannon reached out a fork and scooped up some of the dark chocolate filling and cream. "Yum. She's right."

Kate gave in to temptation and cut and ate a small piece. "Oh yes. I can feel the chocolate dancing in my bloodstream already."

In contrast to the fleet-footed waitress, Hilda's movements were deliberate, almost ponderous. As she emerged slowly from the diner, her gaze fixed on Shannon and Kate, she reminded Shannon of Laura's serious-faced senior portrait. Both had the same air of disregarding life's frivolities. Hilda was much taller and heavier, however, with short, sleek, gray hair. She wore a white apron over practical jeans and a long-sleeve T-shirt.

"Please, join us," Shannon said. She smiled warmly, hoping to influence Hilda to soften a bit. She gave Hilda their names as the woman scraped a chair out from the table and sat, settling herself a little way back, broad, capable hands folded in her lap.

Hilda nodded at the introductions but merely said, "How's the pie?"

"Excellent," Shannon said, taking another bite. "I've never had such flaky, tender piecrust. What's your secret?"

Hilda snorted. "Besides fifty years of making pies, you mean? Ice water, lard, butter, and a dash of vinegar. Then you've got to handle it just enough. Too much and it gets tough."

"I'll keep that in mind. Anyway, we stopped by to say hello. Your niece Laura lives in Apple Grove and works for Kate."

"Yes," Kate said. "At my pet-grooming business. I do dogs, mostly. Wash, dry, clip."

Hilda looked dubious. "Laura, working with animals? She's always been afraid of dogs. Big ones, anyway. She was bitten as a child."

More proof that Hillary and Laura were the same person. "Well, she's doing fine now," Kate said.

"How's she handling that loser's death?" Hilda said. "Gary Booker." She spat his name like it was synonymous with evil. "Strange they both ended up in the same town."

"Apple Grove has a lot to recommend it," Shannon said neutrally.

"Unlike Pine Valley, you mean?" Hilda snapped. "This is a nice little town. Yes, we've had hard times, but we're honest, hardworking people."

Shannon held up a hand. "I totally agree. We've enjoyed meeting everyone here, haven't we, Kate?"

"Oh yes," Kate agreed, her eyes innocently wide. "And we love your pie."

"Thanks," Hilda said, seemingly mollified. "I don't begrudge Laura moving away after Gary pulled what he did. She blamed him for her parents' death, and frankly, so do I."

"I'm sorry for your losses," Shannon murmured. "What exactly did Gary do?"

"Hold on. Would you like more coffee? I think I'll join you."

*   *   *

Hilda liberally doctored her coffee with sugar and milk and stirred vigorously. After taking a big slurp, she said, "Sit back, girls, and rest a spell. I'm going to tell you a story. A few years ago, my sister and her husband were running the tree farm with the help of their only daughter. Oh, they hired hands to help groom the trees and do the cutting and heavy work in season. They weren't rich, but they got by. Even when the recession hit. For this area, it was like a line of dominos." She demonstrated the movement of falling dominos with short flips of her hand. "The housing industry tanked. So the wood orders dried up. Then the lumber mills closed. And the trucking companies went out of business."

She paused for another deep draft of coffee. "Ah. We make a fine cup of coffee here, don't we? Goes perfect with my pies. Anyway, the tree farm was fortunate because even during the worst times, people buy their trees. They might spend less, want to go with a smaller tree, but they're still buying." She paused dramatically. "That's what makes Gary's actions even worse. If he'd never shown up, I firmly believe that my sister and her husband would be alive today. But the stress killed them both." She shook her head.

From Kate's tense expression, Shannon guessed she shared her desire to shake the information out of the woman. Even Boyd was moving restlessly under the table. But Hilda was someone who enjoyed taking advantage of a captive audience, she surmised.

"So," Hilda went on, "Gary came along in response to an ad for help, and before you knew it, the whole family was all 'Gary this' and 'Gary that.'" She gave an indignant snort. "You might've thought he walked on water."

"He did know his way around a tree farm," Shannon felt compelled to say. "At least, his recent employers thought so."

Hilda wagged a stubby finger at Shannon. "That may be so. But nothing gave him the right to talk my brother-in-law into subdividing land and trying to sell residential lots in the worst housing market in living history. It cost him over one hundred thousand dollars, so of course he got a mortgage. One of those horrible adjustable-rate things. But that's not even the worst thing he did."

*   *   *

Esther pulled up a chair on the other side of the table. Although she and Jake were alone in the newspaper office, she lowered her voice to a near whisper. "That man was a criminal. Too bad nobody could prove it."

"Because he talked Roger Jenkins into subdividing?" Jake protested. "It might have been unethical, but that's not a crime."

Esther pursed her lips. "No, young man. He took kick-backs from the contractors who did the site work and built the roads and laid the water pipes. And when Roger found out he was playing both sides of the fence—"

*   *   *

"It killed him," Hilda said. "Roger fell off that barn be-cause he was too upset to watch his footing. That man had been on the roof dozens of times. He wasn't a novice up there, horsing around. No sir."

"Did anyone witness the accident?" Shannon asked, exchanging glances with Kate.

"Only Gary. He was in the barn when it happened."

Great. Another suspicious death. "Laura must have been devastated by all this," Shannon said. "I can't imagine."

"Again, the bad story gets worse. Laura was engaged to Gary. And when he left, it broke her heart."

Now the letter from Laura made sense, Shannon thought. She remembered one of the lines: "I know things didn't work out with the farm the way we hoped, but relationships are for better or worse, right?" Despite the talk of kickbacks, the failure of the housing project, and the death of her father, Laura had still wanted Gary in her life.

Hilda's face was somber. "Laura was so enamored of that man. No one could get through to her, not even her mother. She defended him up and down in the face of all the evidence. But after he ran off and left her holding the bag, it finally seemed to sink in that he was no good." She shook her head sadly. "A woman can forgive almost anything. Except the knowledge that a man never loved you after all."

— 20 —

"**I** think Laura Jenkins did it," Kate said. She swallowed another spoonful of oyster stew, her eyes rolling in ecstasy. "Yum. I'm so glad we stopped here."

Shannon, deep into a bowl of clam chowder, agreed on both counts. After they finished their soup, a buttery crab-melt sandwich to share awaited. Jake, unable to choose just one crustacean, had ordered clam, crab, and shrimp sliders and fries.

Despite the trio's eagerness to get back to Apple Grove, Jake had suggested they stop at Maureen's Seafood, a rustic restaurant overlooking the water along Highway 101. Here, seated in a big, plush booth, they could review what they'd learned and decide upon a strategy in comfort. Full stomachs were essential in all good investigations, he insisted.

"She seems to have the most motive—with the exception of Finn," Shannon said. "From her point of view, it must seem like Gary destroyed her whole life."

"He was certainly involved in the real estate deals," Jake said. "The newspaper articles said that he accompanied Roger Jenkins in presenting the subdivision plans to the town. And the planning board minutes backed that up, with Gary taking questions from the board. I have to admit it was a sound plan. They subdivided only fifty acres of the two hundred, and if the lots had sold, they stood to make back many times the original investment. And I discovered that the property was recorded in a company name, PVF, Inc. That's why we didn't find Roger or Hillary listed in the tax deeds."

"That was great that you were able to get copies of the plans and the property records before the city offices closed," Kate said.

"Yeah, thanks to Esther. She knew someone at city hall who helped me. Gosh, I almost had a heart attack when she found out what I was really up to. She's a pretty sharp cookie. I had to promise to keep them in the loop."

Kate took one of Jake's fries and swirled it through the ketchup. "I have to admit I feel sorry for Laura. All her dreams exploded right in her face. And to lose both her parents so quickly … wow. I mean, I don't see mine that often, but at least they're still on the planet."

"Did Hilda tell you how Hillary died?" Jake picked up the bite of crab melt Kate had cut for him and popped it into his mouth. "Mmm. The cheese makes it."

"She had a heart attack," Shannon said. "And like with too many women, there weren't any early warning signs. Of course, she'd been suffering incredible stress for quite a while."

"And Laura took off soon after?" Jake asked. "I can imagine how hard it was for her, attempting to make a go of the farm alone. Mortgage, taxes, upkeep—owning a farm is expensive, and the margins are thin. No wonder she gave up and let the bank take it."

"Exactly. Her aunt said that soon after the bank foreclosed, she just vanished without telling anyone where she was going or why. Apparently it took her a little while to find Gary. How long had she been in Apple Grove when you hired her, Kate?"

Kate shrugged. "I think she said she had just come to town. I wasn't advertising; she was walking up and down the street, applying for jobs, and she came in one day. I had just decided that I needed an assistant. It seems that everyone wants Christmas pictures with their pets this year, so I've gotten tons of extra grooming appointments."

The waitress came by to refill their coffee and remove the empty dishes. Kate packed a few scraps into a takeout box for Boyd. Then they sat in mutual silence, letting the food and the situation digest.

"So now what?" Jake asked.

"I'll call Chief Grayson when I get back to town," Shannon said. "I'll take him all the information we gathered today as well as the threat and the papers I found in Gary's room." She patted her big leather handbag. "I have copies with me. While nothing is conclusive, maybe it will convince him to continue the investigation."

"You know, if it wasn't for that threat," Jake noted, "we might not have been so inclined to dig. Finn was in jail when you got it, right? So that was a huge mistake on someone's part."

"True," Shannon said. "I only started poking around as a favor to Marge. The case did look all neatly sewed up. Finn had motive, means, and opportunity, and no alibi after he left Carrie's house that morning. He could have come back to the farm through the back fence. That's how the prosecutor is thinking about it, no doubt."

"If only we knew for sure that Laura was at the farm when Gary was killed," Kate said.

"She was," Shannon replied. "She was working there dressed as a snowman."

Jake snapped his fingers. "That's right. I saw the snow-man. That outfit was pretty bulky." He demonstrated with waves of his hands around his midsection. "It looked like there was a wire framework holding it in shape."

"So there was room inside it for a bow and arrow," Kate said with admiration. "How incredibly clever."

The waitress came by again with the coffee pot, but Shannon shook her head. "Check, please. We've got to get on the road."

* * *

South Main Street was quiet when they arrived in Apple Grove. All the stores and most of the eateries were closed for the night, including Paisley Craft Market.

"Looks like everyone is at the skating party," Jake commented. "I should probably head over there and take some photos for my feature."

"Drop me off behind the craft market, please," Shannon said. "I'm parked back there."

"I've forwarded all the photos to your phone," Kate said as they pulled up next to the truck. "Let us know if you need us to come with you to see the chief."

"I'm sure I'll be fine, but thanks." Shannon picked up the manila envelope of paperwork Jake had copied. As she opened the back door of the SUV, Boyd whimpered. "You're a good boy," Shannon cooed, giving his head a pat. "You were so good and patient today on our ride."

"I have an idea," Kate said. "Why don't you take him for the night? You can test out what it's like having a dog around.

See if it works for you—and the twins." Kate guessed that they would be enthusiastic about a pet. As if he understood her, Boyd ratcheted up his whimper to a full-blown whine. They all laughed. "He knows what we're talking about," Kate said. "I've never seen such an intelligent dog."

"That's why he likes Shannon," Jake said. "He's smart."

"All right, you guys," Shannon said with a rueful smile. "You win. I'll take him. For the night, anyway. You're coming with me, Boyd."

Boyd yipped in excitement, making them all laugh again.

After unloading the dog along with his leash and dishes and a bag of food—making Shannon wonder if Kate had planned it all along—Jake and Kate drove off. Shannon unlocked the truck and got herself and Boyd inside before calling the chief.

She called the station first. "Oh, he's not here," the dispatcher told her. "He's over at the skating rink. Community duty." Shannon tried his cell, but he didn't pick up. She didn't bother leaving him a message, deciding she might as well go to the park and find him there. "Come on, Boyd. We're going for a walk."

The park was only a couple of blocks away, and Shannon could hear the festivities well before she arrived on the scene. The lights surrounding the rink created a glow in the night sky, and lively Christmas rock music trumpeted from loudspeakers. As she drew closer, she saw people on skates circling the large rink. Some moved slowly, tentative on their teetering skates, while others whizzed and twirled, showing off their skills. Couples glided arm in arm or holding hands, and she identified Joyce and Bill, ice-dancing as promised.

The crowd was thick outside the rink too, with bystanders

milling around, eating food from the vending trucks, and visiting with friends. Savory scents of grilling meat and hot grease drifted on the frosty air.

Shannon paused on the edge of the throng, searching for the chief's familiar profile. There. Over on the other side of the rink. She recognized the stalwart, watchful pose of a policeman. If he wasn't Grayson, he'd know where he was.

"Shannon!" a voice cried. Turning to look, she spotted Essie pushing through the crowd, a pair of skates slung over her shoulder. She wore a cute skating outfit of a red wool jacket, a short plaid skirt, and tights. "You're back. And you have a new friend with you." She reached down and patted Boyd.

"Yes, he's going to be my overnight guest. Don't ask. You're skating, I take it?"

"Just finished." Essie scanned the crowd with a troubled expression. "Carrie came with me, but now I can't find her. She said she was going to get us something to eat, but she's nowhere near the food trucks."

"Maybe she's in the restroom." A short distance away was the low brick building that served as changing room and bathrooms.

Essie frowned. "No, that's where I was when I lost her. When I went in, she was talking to that kid from the farm. When I came out, she was gone."

Shannon thought of Laura and a little alarm went off in her head. There was no reason for her to be a threat to Carrie—was there? "Kid from the farm?"

Essie shrugged. "Tom. Or is it Tim? You know, the one who works with Chaz."

That's OK, then. She changed the topic. "Do you happen to know what happened with Finn's hearing?"

"He made bail this afternoon."

Shannon felt a rush of relief. "That's great. He'll be home for Christmas." No matter how speedy the court system was, the trial wouldn't happen until after the holidays. That would give Finn plenty of time to rebuild the relationship with his parents. And perhaps with her new evidence, the charges would be dropped entirely. "I've got to get going, Essie. If I see Carrie, I'll have her call you."

"Thanks. I guess I'll head on home. Have a good night."

Essie disappeared into the crowd, and Shannon continued to make her way to where the police officer was stationed. As she drew closer, she saw with a pang of disappointment that it was Brownley. She wasn't going to talk to anyone but the chief.

"Hi, Officer Brownley. Is the chief around?"

Brownley, too distracted by the civilians under his watch to spare Shannon more than a glance, shook his head. "Nope. He was here, but he was just called out to an accident."

Maybe that's why he hadn't answered his cell. He was out of range. "Well, if you see him before I do, tell him I'm looking for him. It's about Gary Booker, and it's important."

Now she had his attention. He swung his big head her way and grinned. "Didn't you hear? We closed the book on that one already. Ha. Closed the book on Booker. Hate to admit it, but you and Stone helped with your poking around the farm." Smirking, he gave her an ironic thumbs-up before turning his attention back to the rink, where a gaggle of awkward teens shrieked and giggled as they wobbled past.

Shannon sighed and turned to go. Obviously she wasn't going to catch up with the chief tonight. She might as well go home and organize the information, print out the photos, and pull together a package to give him tomorrow. Finn was out of jail, so there was no urgency anyway.

She was halfway home when her cell rang. She snatched it up, hoping it was the chief. Instead, she heard a scratchy, muffled woman's voice. "Shannon? Shannon?"

The connection was terrible—crackling and spotty. Her senses went on alert. "Yes, this is Shannon."

"I need your help." The woman began to sniffle and sob. "At the farm."

"Is this Marge?"

More sobs.

"You should call the police. Have you called them?"

The phone went dead and Shannon dropped it into her lap. What was going on? What could have happened? Had Finn snapped and hurt Marge and Dick? Dread trickled through her veins, making her palms sweat inside her gloves.

Shannon slowed and entered a side road. "Hang on, Boyd," she said to the dog. "We're going to the farm." She turned around and sped back toward town. She'd told Marge to call the police, but she had better do it. She called the station, but due to the hour, the dispatcher was now off duty and her call was forwarded to central dispatch at the county.

"What's the nature of your emergency?"

"I don't know exactly," Shannon admitted. She repeated what Marge had said. "That's all she said."

"So she could just be upset about something? Call your local law enforcement. And call back if there's an emergency."

Once again Shannon tried the chief's cell, and once again she got his voice mail. She told him to come to the farm immediately, that it was urgent. Then she called the twins at home. Alec answered.

"I'm going to be late," she said. "I have to go out to the farm. What are you and Lara doing?" She kept her tone light, not wanting to alarm him unnecessarily.

"A few of our friends came over, and we're playing board games, and we have a fire going in the fireplace. It's awesome."

Shannon pictured the happy, cozy scene and wished she were there right now, joining in the fun and laughter. Instead, she was heading into a cold, dark night to face who knew what.

"We saved you some dinner," Alec went on. "We weren't sure if you'd eaten on the way back."

"We did, but thanks. See you soon."

All was quiet at the farm. The parking lot was empty except for a couple of cars and the farm pickup parked next to the barn. A porch light shone next to the farmhouse front door; otherwise, the house was dark. Inside the barn, a light was on and she heard the blare of rock music.

Leaving Boyd in the truck with the window down, she went to the front door anyway and knocked. She peered through a window into the dark parlor. No one was in there, and the fireplace was cold. Then she went around to the back door and looked inside the kitchen. One light burned over the sink, and she could see a cat curled up in the rocking chair, Marge's knitting draped over the arm. Where was she? Where were Finn and Dick? She'd expected to stumble upon a scene of anger and recrimination. Instead, they didn't appear to be home.

So who had called? She hadn't recognized the number and had assumed it was a cellphone.

She thought about calling out, but some instinct warned her to be quiet despite the music playing. Instead, she crept toward the barn. Careful to remain out of view, she peered through a crack in the wide sliding door.

In the open space in the center of the barn, Hillary—that is, Laura—stood facing her, a furious expression distorting her face. She wasn't wearing her glasses, Shannon noticed. Instinctively, she shrank back, but then, after a moment, she realized the woman couldn't see her. Her attention was entirely focused on a young man who had his back to Shannon and was dressed in a cap and winter coat.

Laura's foot lashed out and kicked over the blaring boom box, pulling the cord out of the socket. The music blessedly stopped.

"Hey. What'd you do that for?" He ran to the box and knelt down beside it. Shannon recognized him. Tim. The other helper here at the farm. *What had Essie said? That Carrie was talking to Tim.*

"I can't hear myself think with that racket," Laura said.

"It helps me relax," Tim muttered. He pushed the buttons to make sure they still worked, then wrapped the cord around the radio. "I can't do it."

"You can't back out now. Once she's gone and Finn's in jail, this place will be ours. Piece of cake."

"But you want me to kill her! I didn't sign up for that." He stood, the boom box tucked under his arm, and turned away.

Laura ran to Tim and grabbed his arm, tugging him back. "It's too late, stupid," she scoffed. "You kidnapped her.

That's life in prison already." She lowered her voice slightly. "Listen to me. If we follow my plan, we'll get away with it. No one will ever know. I promise."

They must have Carrie stashed somewhere. But where? The house or sheds or barn? Or even among the trees? The farm was huge, and she could be anywhere. *If only the chief would arrive!* But she couldn't depend on that.

I need to find Carrie. Now.

— 21 —

"**G**o to jail!" Alec cried. "Not again!" He threw down his card in mock anger.

Lara and the others burst into laughter. "I can't believe I'm beating you for once," Lara said. The phone in the hall rang loudly, interrupting. "I'll get it." She jumped up from her cross-legged position on the rug in front of the fire and dashed out of the room.

She snatched up the phone on the fifth ring. "Hello," she said, breathless.

"Lara? It's Michael. How are you enjoying your vacation?"

"It's been awesome so far. Tonight we're playing Monopoly with friends. Are you calling from Japan?"

"Yes, I am. It's about noon here. Is your mother around?"

"No, she isn't. Have you tried her cell?"

"I did. It went right to voice mail."

"That's weird. She called a while ago and said she had to go out to the farm."

"The tree farm? Did she say why?"

"I don't think so. Alec took the call. I can ask him."

"No, that's OK. Have a good night, Lara. I hope to be home soon."

"I hope so too, Michael." Her gaze fell on the tall tree he had helped her mother pick out, and she admired the twinkling lights and the colorful ornaments nestled amid the branches. "You should see the tree! It's fantastic."

"I know. Your mother texted me a picture of it."

"She did? Wow. Way to go, Mum. Anyway, I'll tell her you called."

Almost five thousand miles away, Michael put his phone in his pocket and continued along the path winding through the Imperial Garden's traditional Japanese landscapes. He was sharply disappointed that he hadn't reached Shannon. He'd waited until eight o'clock Oregon time so the shop would be closed and dinnertime over. Instead of relaxing at home, she had gone out to that blasted farm again. Why? He stopped dead in the middle of the path, annoying a group of American tourists clustered behind him. After stepping aside, he pulled out his phone and made another call.

*   *   *

Careful not to crunch her feet on the gravel of the parking lot, Shannon eased away from the barn door. As she stood indecisively, not sure of her next move, she heard a faint banging beyond the barn. Running softly toward the sound, she soon figured out it was coming from the small, battered sedan parked next to the farm pickup. The trunk. Carrie must be in the trunk. Another thump resounded from inside, along with a muffled "Help!"

Praying that the doors weren't locked, Shannon lunged for the driver's side. *Whew.* It was open. She crouched down, her left hand searching blindly for the trunk release. There. She heard the pop of the lock. She dashed back around the car and lifted the trunk.

Lying in a curled-up position, Carrie cowered, her arms

over her face. "It's OK, Carrie. It's me, Shannon." Shannon reached in, tugging gently on her arm. "Come on, we need to get out of here."

Carrie moved her arms away from her head and pushed herself to a half-sitting position. She blinked. "Shannon? Shannon!"

"Hush. They're in the barn." Shannon helped her swing her legs over the edge and climb out. As Carrie tottered to a standing position, she winced and put a hand to the back of her head. Her cellphone, hidden among her clothes, clattered to the ground.

"Did they hit you?"

Carrie nodded, swaying on her feet. Thankful for inept criminals, Shannon scooped up the phone and put an arm around Carrie's shoulders. It wasn't far to the truck, but they'd have to cross right in front of the barn. They could make it if they hurried.

They were near the door when the arguing escalated. "I'm not doing it, and that's final!" Tim shouted.

"Why not?" Laura's tone was casual, persuasive. "Like I said, it will look like an accident. Put her out in the field, and overnight, she'll just slip away. A nice case of hypothermia after falling and hitting her head. But you'd better hurry. The Olsons will be home soon."

Shannon felt a rush of relief. The Olsons weren't lying dead somewhere. They just weren't home.

"You're crazy!" Tim yelled. "Out of your mind! Insane! Do it yourself! I'm out of here! In fact, I think I'll go to the police. I'll get off if I testify against you. Right?" He laughed.

A piercing shriek of rage was followed by a loud thunk. Shannon and Carrie froze.

"I guess I'll do it myself," Laura said in a deadly tone.

Shannon's instincts told her to turn around and find somewhere to hide. Laura would be coming out of the barn any second. She pulled Carrie around and headed as quickly as possible the other way, given Carrie's stumbling gait. Maybe they could circle through the trees and around the house to the truck.

Too late. The big door rattled along its tracks and Shannon sensed Laura's presence behind them. "Oh, nice. Two for the price of one," she said. Despite her outburst a moment before, her tone was again calm.

She must be insane. Sane people didn't flip-flop between anger and icy control. Shannon picked up the pace, hunching her shoulders against Laura's attack. If they could get beyond the vehicles into the trees, they had a chance. It would be easy to get lost in there, and they just had to hold out long enough for the police to arrive.

If they ever did.

Shannon heard the whistle of an arrow as it flew past her head. She pulled Carrie along, forcing her to run or fall flat. "Come on, Carrie. You can do it."

"You might as well give up," Laura called. "I'm going to hunt you down." She gave an eerie, gleeful laugh that made Shannon's hair stand up on the back of her neck.

They ducked behind the pickup as another arrow pinged against the metal. "You should have minded your own business, Shannon! I've got plenty more where this came from." A crack as an arrow hit the truck window. "And I'm a great shot, as I'm sure you both know, thanks to your snooping. I'm also good with a knife."

A knife? Shannon's heart sank. If Laura got within striking distance with a knife, they were done for.

Another few feet and they were among the trees. Shannon didn't follow the aisle between rows; she cut sideways, forcing their way through trees growing closely together. She tried to keep their noise to a minimum, and thanks to good upkeep, there were few sticks to crack and reveal their movements.

Then Carrie tripped over a short stump. Despite Shannon's attempt to catch her, she thumped to the ground flat on her face. "Ow!" she cried involuntarily.

Suddenly Laura was there, panting, the whites of her eyes glinting in the starlight. In her hand, she clutched a bow. She threw it aside and reached for the sheath hanging from her belt. The knife.

In the distance, Boyd let out yips of distress. Did he sense something bad was happening? Shannon found herself raising two fingers to her mouth to do something she hadn't for years. She whistled—long, loud, and ear-piercing.

"I don't know what good you think that will do you," Laura sneered. "No one's within miles of here." Knife drawn and ready to slash, Laura advanced on them, her legs wide in a primal stance.

"You don't want to do this," Shannon said, struggling to keep her voice calm.

Laura gave that maniacal laugh again. "Gary deserved to die. Why couldn't you just leave things alone?" She raised the knife and charged at Shannon.

A yellow flash flew through the air and hit Laura right in the back, making the knife fly out of her hand. Boyd. He began to growl and nip at her thick jacket. Laura shrieked. "Get him off me! Help! He's going to kill me!"

Carrie sat up. "Maybe we should let him do that."

Laura shrieked louder.

Shannon unclipped the leash still attached to Boyd's collar. "Down, boy," she said, and he immediately stopped growling and moved aside. Shannon took the length of strong webbing and tied Laura's hands. "Don't move, or I'll set him on you again."

"That dog must be part police dog," Carrie said with admiration. "I've never seen anything like that."

Boyd lay down beside her and panted, acting like his heroics were all in a day's work. He continued to watch Laura closely though, his ears perking up whenever she twitched.

"I think I'll keep him." Shannon surprised herself with her sudden decision. "I mean, how can I give up a dog who saved my life? And yours."

Shannon had just pulled Carrie's phone out to call again for help when they heard the crunch of tires on the gravel road, accompanied by the flash of headlights in the treetops. A second vehicle arrived. Car doors slammed, and shortly after, flickering flashlights moved across the driveway.

Shannon gave Carrie an exuberant hug. "The police are here." Relief sang in her veins. They were safe, Gary's murderer had been found, and Finn would go free. She stood and shouted back, directing the officers to her location.

*   *   *

A couple of hours later, Chief Grayson finally allowed Shannon to leave, accompanied by the faithful Boyd.

Walking away, a thought blazed into her head. She had never gotten through to Grayson, so what tipped him off.

"How did you know to come out here, Chief?"

"I got a really long distance call from some guy in Tokyo." Grayson grinned. "He thought you might need a hand."

Shannon was now officially drained, fatigued, and wrung out by a long and harrowing day. With gratitude, she loaded the dog into Old Blue and headed home, into the cold night lit only by a swath of glittering stars.

Events hadn't slowed after Laura's capture. Quite the opposite. The Olsons, including Finn, returned from visiting relatives just as the police escorted Shannon, Carrie, and Laura to the parking lot. Although stunned by Laura's guilt, they were jubilant and overjoyed at the proof of Finn's innocence. The sight of Finn hugging his parents while all three cried would stay with Shannon for a very long time.

Next, two ambulances screamed their arrival to take Tim, concussed from Laura's attack with a shovel, and Carrie to the hospital. Carrie claimed to be feeling all right, but Chief Grayson insisted she be checked out.

Laura, confronted by the reality of her arrest, babbled a confession that took both Brownley and Doan to document. Yes, she had followed Gary to Apple Grove with plans to kill him for destroying her life. In addition, she blamed him for the death of her parents. She'd shot Gary after hiding a bow in her snowman outfit as Jake had guessed, and later had stolen Finn's arrows to frame him.

Tim was interested both in running the farm and getting revenge on Gary. Gary had not only hit on Tim's girlfriend, Amy, but he had asked her out the night Gary and

Carrie had broken up at the inn. The day of the murder, Tim neglected to tell anyone that Gary had gone to fix the fence. He also kept people away from that area of the farm while Laura stalked Gary. Overzealous and impulsive, Tim had given Shannon the threatening note without Laura's knowledge.

After Carrie started poking around, Laura decided to kill her but make it look like an accident. With Finn in jail, Laura planned to become the Olsons' surrogate daughter and take over the farm. She considered it just recompense for her losses.

Shannon gave Jake's manila envelope to Grayson and made her official statement. Thankfully, the Olson kitchen was deemed an adequate site, and she hadn't had to go to the station. At their insistence, she also handed over her cellphone so the police could download photographs of the documents they had found in Pine Valley.

But before she relinquished her phone, she sent two texts. One was to Michael: "We're safe. The snowman—Gary's ex—did it. Talk to you tomorrow? Miss you." The second was to Jake and Kate: "Laura confessed. Exclusive interview tomorrow?"

As she pulled Old Blue to a stop in the mansion's drive, Shannon felt a final release of tension. The case was solved, and now she could focus on getting ready for the holidays. She reached out and patted Boyd, who gazed at her with big, brown, trusting eyes. "Ready to go and check out your new home? I think there might be a treat waiting for you. You certainly deserve one tonight."

— 22 —

The blended voices of choir and congregation created a gorgeous, uplifting harmony as they moved into the stirring refrain of "O Holy Night": *Fall on your knees! O hear the angel voices!* Shannon's heart soared as she sang the moving words of the old carol, words that perfectly expressed the wondrous worship on this holiest of nights, Christmas Eve.

First Methodist Church was suitably decked for the occasion, with candles glowing in the stained glass windows and evergreens decorating the pews and altar rail. Large red poinsettias were clustered in front of the altar, where more candles burned. On the opposite side of the church from the choir stood an almost life-size Nativity set, the empty cradle awaiting the arrival of baby Jesus.

The pews were packed, parishioners and their guests dressed in their finest suits and dresses. Shannon sat on the aisle with Alec, Lara, Beth, and Deborah seated beside her. Sharing the pew were Joyce and Bill and their two daughters and their daughters' fiancés. Joyce would have her hands full with two weddings next summer!

But with a little squeezing, one more person could fit in their row. Someone who apparently wasn't going to arrive in time: Michael. Last time she'd talked to him, a couple of days ago, he was still trying to make it home before Christmas. He had only one hour until that deadline. But despite her disappointment, how lucky she was to be spending Christmas with her loved ones. Tomorrow was going to be perfect.

The song ended, and with a rustle of clothing, everyone sat. Shannon gazed around the beautiful church, the flickering candlelight giving it an otherworldly atmosphere. Just about everyone she knew in Apple Grove was here tonight. On the other side of the church, she spotted Carrie seated with the Olsons, next to Finn. Perhaps once the wounds inflicted by Gary Booker's life and death healed, Finn and Carrie would find happiness together. She hoped so.

The lovely service went on, through the homily and prayers and favorite carols, and culminated in the special event everyone was waiting for: lighting of the personal candles. As everyone began to sing "Silent Night," ushers scurried up front and lit theirs from the main candle on the altar, then passed the flame to parishioners. One by one, candles flickered into life along the pews, moving up to where Shannon stood—a perfect illustration of passing the light from one soul to another.

Just as Alec lit Shannon's candle, she heard someone behind her say, "Is there room for one more?" She turned to see Michael next to the pew, a grin on his tired face. He clutched a candle in his hand.

"Absolutely," she said, her heart leaping for joy. She gestured for everyone to slide down. Michael moved in beside her, so close that his shoulder touched hers. He smelled of fresh, cold air and that indefinable Michael scent that she so adored. With a hand that trembled slightly, she touched her flame to his candle's wick. As the flame caught and held, her eyes met his in a long, silent communion that said everything.

Glories stream from Heaven afar, Heavenly hosts sing alleluia.

Indeed.

*   *   *

Christmas morning dawned clear and cold, a deepening blue sky arching over the snow-covered hills and valleys and streets of Apple Grove. Wood smoke drifted from chimneys as lights popped on all over town, children up early and eager to see what Santa had brought them.

At The Apple Grove Inn, Betty and Tom rose at daybreak to prepare their trademark breakfast strata made with eggs, ham, and multicolored peppers for their guests. Homemade sticky buns, hickory-smoked bacon and sausage, and fruit salad rounded out the menu. Normally Gertrude helped, but she was spending Christmas at Shannon's with her sister, Deborah. After setting everything up in warmer trays in the main dining room, they went back to their quarters, Tom lugging a tray for the family.

The cries and squeals of grandchildren greeted them along with more subdued hellos from the children's parents, lounging around the living room and nursing big mugs of coffee.

"Can we open presents now?" one little boy asked.

Tom set the tray down on the big dining table. "Of course. Everyone, help yourself when you're ready."

With whoops of excitement, the children dove for the presents under the big tree. Betty poured herself a cup of coffee and sat on a love seat to watch. Seeing the children's excitement brought back memories of when her three were little. By the fond looks on their faces, she realized they were reliving those days too.

Tom sat beside her and held her hand. "Isn't this fantastic?" he said. "All of us together on Christmas." He squeezed her hand. "We have a wonderful family, Mrs. Russo."

She leaned over and gave him a kiss on the cheek. "Yes, we do, Mr. Russo."

Over at Joyce and Bill's, proceedings were much more sedate. After the exchange of gifts, Kelly and Phoebe Buchanan sat with Joyce on one of the wide, plush sofas, drinking coffee and discussing wedding plans. The girls, opposite in every way, wanted totally different weddings too. Phoebe was content with a backyard wedding with friends and family, while Kelly wanted the whole two-hundred-guest extravaganza at the church and country club. As independent adults, both were alike in one particular: They planned to pay most of the expenses. Joyce, seated between her lovely daughters, marveled at their beauty and personality. They'd chosen their partners well, and Joyce hugged herself at the thought that, perhaps someday soon, there would be grandchildren.

Kelly's fiancé was an avid golfer, and he had Bill and Phoebe's betrothed practicing putting shots on the carpet with his new putter. One of Joyce's cats was very interested in the ball and kept batting it under the Christmas tree, much to the amusement of the women.

At yet another Apple Grove home, Melanie Burkhart and her son, Greg, slept in. They were going to Shannon's for Christmas dinner, along with Greg's fiancée and her widower father, who would be arriving from Portland in the late morning.

"So what's Samantha's father like?" Melanie asked Greg when he stumbled into the kitchen looking for coffee.

"He's nice," he said, gazing out into the backyard at the birds darting around the feeders. "He's a botany professor at Portland Community College." He threw a sly glance at his pretty, dark-haired mother. "Good-looking too. Tall and blond, like Sam." Hmm. A handsome botany professor. Melanie thought about the wool trousers she'd planned to wear and decided instead upon a black velvet skirt paired with a green silk blouse. Much more festive, right? After all, it was Christmas.

Meanwhile, in the big kitchen at the Paisley mansion, the smell of roasting goose filled the air as Beth opened the oven door to baste the golden birds. Deborah peeled potatoes, Gertrude prepared side vegetables, and Shannon stirred a big vat of cock-a-leekie soup. All the women wore festive dresses covered by white bib aprons. Boyd was in what had become his favorite spot under the big table, chewing on the rawhide bone Santa had brought him.

"What's in that soup?" Gertrude asked.

"Chicken, rice, and leeks. It's a traditional Scottish soup."

"I'll have to try it at the inn. It sounds perfect for our winter menu."

"I can email you the recipe on my new iPad," Deborah offered. Shannon and the twins had bought it for her since the older woman was enjoying the Internet so much.

Lara wandered into the kitchen. "I finished setting the table."

"Thank you. Where's Alec?" Shannon asked.

"He finished shoveling the walk, and now he's messing with our snowboards." Shannon had given the twins snowboarding boots and boards for Christmas, much to their delight. In turn, they had given her subscriptions to a couple of mystery book clubs, hoping that in the future, she would merely read about murders rather than solve them. "What can I do now?" Lara asked.

"How about putting together the smoked-salmon platter?" Shannon suggested. "Guests will be arriving soon, and it'd be nice to have that ready."

Deborah put a big pot of potatoes on to boil and said, "Good thing we have such a large stove." Indeed, every one of the six burners was soon put to use heating gravy and vegetables and the gently steaming Christmas pudding.

Alec poked his head into the kitchen. "Mum, can I have your help for a minute?"

Relinquishing her spoon to Gertrude, Shannon followed Alec to the dining room, Lara tagging along. "What is it?" she asked as they entered, looking around. Everything on the table and sideboard appeared ready for the fifteen who would dine that day. Alec nodded toward the other doorway, the one leading to the big entrance hall. Michael stood there, blue eyes twinkling, handsome in a tweed sport coat and gray trousers. He wore a jaunty red-and-gray argyle sweater underneath the jacket. "Michael! I didn't hear you arrive." She went to greet him.

"Merry Christmas, Shannon." He put his hands on her shoulders.

"Merry Christmas to you too." Behind her, Lara giggled. She followed Michael's gaze up to the top of the doorway. A large sprig of mistletoe hung there. "What—!" Her exclamation was cut off as Michael pulled her into his arms and kissed her firmly—a deep, warm, thrilling kiss that almost made her toes curl.

After several long, delicious moments, he pulled back and smiled. "Let's try this again later," he whispered. "Without the mistletoe and the audience." He cocked an eyebrow toward Alec and Lara, who dashed out of the dining room, Lara still giggling in glee.

"I'd like that," Shannon said, crushing him in a hug. The doorbell rang. "Alas, duty calls."

Soon the rest of the guests arrived, and everyone spent an enjoyable social hour in the drawing room, where a large fire roared. Included were Kate and Jake, elderly neighbors Tippy and Wyatt, Melanie and Greg, his fiancée, Samantha, and Sam's charming father, Daniel. Boyd made the rounds, creating new friendships and renewing old ones. More than one cracker from the salmon tray "accidentally" fell to the floor in front of his nose.

At Shannon's invitation, the gang traipsed into the dining room to enjoy the Christmas feast. At each place was a Christmas cracker, sent by Coleen, Shannon's Scottish friend. These paper "firecrackers" were pulled apart with snaps and bangs, releasing paper crowns, jokes, and silly little gifts—whistles and horns and tops and toy cars. The table was alive with laughter and toots and whistles during the soup course. Deborah and Gertrude carried in the geese, golden brown and dripping with rich juices. Michael carved and Shannon, Lara, and Beth passed bowls of whipped potatoes, gravy, green bean casserole, and glazed carrots. Alec led grace and everyone dug in.

"This is fantastic," Kate said, her paper crown sliding down over one eye. "Who knew goose was so tasty?"

"The secret is in the basting," Beth said, going on to explain her method.

"What did you get for a board?" Jake asked Alec.

"Burton Special Edition."

"Great choice. Want to try it out tomorrow? I'm heading up to the ski area."

"I understand you teach botany," Melanie said to Daniel. "I'm a floral designer."

Greg and Samantha held hands under the table. Madly in love, they spent more time gazing into each other's eyes than eating.

Deborah and Gertrude engaged Tippy in a discussion of Apple Grove's bygone days, reminiscing about mutual friends. Wyatt secretly fed Boyd scraps, once in a while calling him "Daisy" after his own old dog, long gone now. Boyd didn't seem to mind.

Lara could have burst with happiness. Her mum was just glowing after that kiss. Michael was awesome, and with any luck, he would someday be her stepfather. After all she'd been through, Mum deserved to be happy. She also adored having her grandmother staying here at the mansion. Beth had almost cried when she'd seen the angel ornaments together again. Mum seemed to have warmed up to her quite a bit.

Seated next to Michael, Shannon brimmed with joy and satisfaction at how well the dinner was going. Judging by the happy chatter and rapid rate of food consumption, they were all having the time of their lives.

After the contents of the serving dishes were decimated and all the guests sat back, groaning with satiety and satisfaction, Lara and Alec cleared the table.

"We have a surprise," Shannon announced, "so everyone stay put."

In the kitchen, Deborah slid the round, dark, fruit-studded pudding out of its container and onto a platter edged with a holly design. Gertrude poured warm homemade custard into a white ceramic pitcher. Shannon brought out a bottle of brandy and poured some into a ladle. Then she doused the pudding. "Bring the matches," she said.

As Shannon entered the dining room, proudly carrying the pudding, Lara turned off the lights. Shannon set the pudding in front of Beth.

"A Christmas pudding!" Beth exclaimed. "I haven't had one in years."

Deborah handed Shannon the matches and she lit the pudding, causing a blue flame to flicker and glow as the brandy burned off. Everyone oohed and aahed.

"That's an interesting tradition," Michael noted. "Setting fire to dessert."

"Yeah, bring on the fire extinguisher," Jake joked.

"We won't need one of those," Shannon said. She handed Beth the serving knife. "Will you do the honors, Mum?"

Beth caught her breath. Alec and Lara exchanged smiles. Beth reached out and took Shannon's hand, squeezing it. "You called me 'Mum,'" she said. "I couldn't have asked for a better Christmas gift."

"Love you, Mum," Shannon whispered, blinking back tears.

"I love you too, Shannon."

Everyone at the table, whether or not they understood the significance of this exchange, was silent, caught in the magical moment. The years of bitterness from what Shannon had taken as abandonment had finally and completely dissipated, like the brandy in the pudding. She had been through a lot in the past couple of years since she was reunited with her mother. She now understood, both from the head and the heart, why Beth had left her and her father in Scotland. Shannon knelt beside Beth, folding her in an embrace.

Kate, sensing the need to pull the crowd's attention from mother and daughter, raised her glass of water and called out, "Cheers for the Christmas pudding!"

They all raised their glasses in a toast. The flames died down, and Beth began to serve slices while Gertrude added custard and passed plates.

Jake, carried away by the excitement, cried out in an imitation of Tiny Tim, "God bless us, every one!" He fervently dug into his helping of pudding.

Around the table, the others, almost in unison, echoed, "God bless us, every one!"

Leaning back in the circle of Michael's arm with Boyd's head resting on her knee, Shannon gazed around the room at her dear family, friends, and neighbors. *Oh yes*, she thought. *I am truly blessed beyond measure!*